From the desk of
Patrick Elliott, CEO

Shane,

Hard to believe it has been a year since I started this competition to name my successor. The family thought—and still thinks—I'm crazy to pit you all against each other, brother against brother against sister. But here we stand, at the finish line. And there can be only one winner.

The final reports are in. The profit margins have been tabulated for all the magazines, and I hold in my hand the name of the new CEO of Elliott Publication Holdings.

If you want to know who it is, come to my office tonight at seven. If you've got the guts...

Patrick

Dear Reader,

Being asked to be a part of a continuity series for the Silhouette Desire line is a real treat. Being asked to write the last book in a series is both a challenge and a treat.

Beyond the Boardroom, the final book in the Elliott family continuity, was great fun to write. I love the idea of setting a book in New York City at Christmastime. And I absolutely adored my hero, Shane. He's so focused on his job for the family company, he never notices the one woman—Rachel Adler—who has been keeping his world in order for years. Until Rachel does the unthinkable and actually quits her job.

I hope you have all enjoyed reading about the Elliotts as much as the twelve of us did writing the books.

And until next time, I wish you good books, great joy and always, more time to read!

Love,

Maureen

P.S. Don't miss my newest release, NEVERMORE, available February 2007 from the Silhouette Nocturne line.

MAUREEN CHILD

BEYOND THE BOARDROOM

Published by Silhouette Books
America's Publisher of Contemporary Romance

For my husband, Mark, because really, all of my books
should be dedicated to him. I love you, honey!

Acknowledgments
Special thanks and acknowledgment are given to
Maureen Child for her contribution to
THE ELLIOTTS continuity.

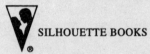 SILHOUETTE BOOKS

ISBN-13: 978-0-373-76765-6
ISBN-10:   0-373-76765-X

BEYOND THE BOARDROOM

Visit Silhouette Books at www.eHarlequin.com

Printed in U.S.A.

MAUREEN CHILD

is a California native who loves to travel. Every chance they get, she and her husband are taking off on another research trip. The author of more than sixty books, Maureen loves a happy ending and still swears that she has the best job in the world. She lives in Southern California with her husband, two children, and a golden retriever with delusions of grandeur.

THE ELLIOTTS

Patrick m. Maeve O'Grady

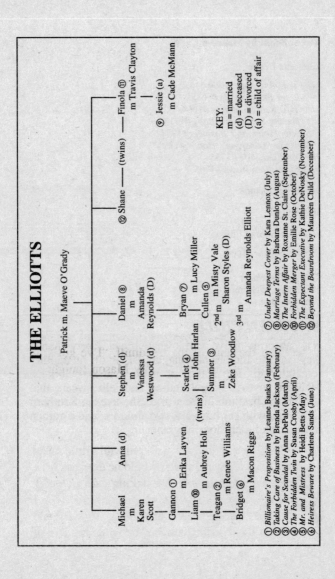

Michael
m
Karen
Scott

Gannon ①
m Erika Layven

Liam ⑩   (twins)
m Aubrey Holt

Teagan ②
m Renee Williams

Bridget ⑥
m Macon Riggs

Anna (d)

Scarlet ④
m John Harlan

Summer ③
m
Zeke Woodlow

Stephen (d)
m
Vanessa
Westwood (d)

Daniel ⑧
m
Amanda
Reynolds (D)

Bryan ⑦
m Lucy Miller

Cullen ⑤
2nd m Misty Vale
Sharon Styles (D)
3rd m
Amanda Reynolds Elliott

⑫ Shane ———— (twins) ———— Finola ⑪
m Travis Clayton

⑨ Jessie (a)
m Cade McMann

KEY:

m = married
(d) = deceased
(D) = divorced
(a) = child of affair

① *Billionaire's Proposition* by Leanne Banks (January)
② *Taking Care of Business* by Brenda Jackson (February)
③ *Cause for Scandal* by Anna DePalo (March)
④ *The Forbidden Twin* by Susan Crosby (April)
⑤ *Mr. and Mistress* by Heidi Betts (May)
⑥ *Heiress Beware* by Charlene Sands (June)
⑦ *Under Deepest Cover* by Kara Lennox (July)
⑧ *Marriage Terms* by Barbara Dunlop (August)
⑨ *The Intern Affair* by Roxanne St. Claire (September)
⑩ *Forbidden Merger* by Emilie Rose (October)
⑪ *The Expectant Executive* by Kathie DeNosky (November)
⑫ *Beyond the Boardroom* by Maureen Child (December)

One

"Okay then," Rachel Adler said, keeping her voice pitched to be heard over the thumping of running feet and the hum of the treadmill. "I've got you booked for dinner with Tawny Mason tonight at eight."

"At Une Nuit?" Shane Elliott asked, reaching for his water bottle, tucked beneath the cord at the head of the machine.

"Where else?" Rachel muttered with a little shake of her head. Why in heaven would he even ask? she wondered. Hadn't she been taking care of every detail of Shane's life for four years now?

"Good." Shane took a long drink of water and Rachel's gaze locked on the bobbing motion of his Adam's apple. Seriously, even the man's *neck* was sexy.

When he'd finished off the last of the water, he wiped sweat from his face with the towel looped around his neck and tossed Rachel the empty bottle. "And call ahead. Have Stash order in some flowers for, um…" He waved one hand in a silent attempt for help.

"Tawny," Rachel provided dryly as she set the empty bottle down on the floor beside her. For heaven's sake, the man couldn't even remember his date's name.

Plus, he knew as well as she did that Stash Martin, manager of Une Nuit, never missed a beat when getting the Elliott family table ready. There would, she knew, be flowers, champagne and some delicious appetizers just waiting for Shane and Tawny.

Tawny.

What kind of woman named her daughter Tawny? A stage mother, hoping for a starlet daughter? Or had the woman taken one look at her newborn baby girl and decided…future bimbo?

"Right." Shane nodded. "Tawny. She says her mother named her for the color of her eyes."

Rachel rolled her own green eyes.

Shane grinned at her and Rachel's stomach did a quick dip and spin.

If she could have managed it without looking like a complete idiot, she'd have kicked her own ass. Honestly. Why was it Shane Elliott who could turn her insides to mush with a simple smile?

The first three years she'd worked with the man, everything had been fine between them. They'd had a good working relationship and Shane even appreciated Rachel's sometimes quirky sense of humor, when most of her previous employers hadn't. Then she'd had to go and ruin the whole thing by falling for him.

For the last year she'd suffered silently, wanting him every day, dreaming about him at night, all the while knowing that he thought of her only as Good ol' Rachel.

Idiot.

"What do you think?" he asked, clearly oblivious to her thoughts. "Roses?"

"Huh?" She blinked, shook her head and reminded herself to concentrate on the moment. "Right. Flowers. Roses are boring."

"Really?"

"Trust me."

"I always do," he said, giving her another of those smiles that had the power to zap an unwary female at twenty paces.

She couldn't do this much longer, she thought. Couldn't keep working with him every day and dying a little more every day. Couldn't set up his dates with other women and imagine him in bed with every one of them. Couldn't keep wasting her life away waiting for the wrong man to wake up and stumble on her.

Sighing, Rachel flipped through her memo book, scanned the notes she kept on the legions of Shane's women and found what she was looking for. "Tawny prefers daisies."

"Sure, I remember now. Such a simple girl."

"Simple*ton*, you mean," she muttered again, keeping her voice low enough that her boss's running feet would drown out the comment.

"What was that?"

"Nothing." She automatically handed him the second bottle of water she'd brought with her to the executive area of the company gym on the fifth floor.

"Rachel, what would I do without you?" he mused, not really expecting an answer.

But oh boy, could she give him one. Rachel was Shane's right hand at *The Buzz,* one of the magazines in the Elliott family empire. As a weekly entertainment magazine, *The Buzz* covered all the new movies, did interviews with up-and-coming directors and fawned over whichever actor or actress was the current hot topic. And as editor in chief of *The Buzz*, Shane did his best to keep on top of everything going on around him.

Of course, when she'd first come to work for him, he hadn't been so involved. Instead he'd tried to avoid the office as much as humanly possible. But slowly, Rachel had convinced him to enjoy his job more.

Back then, he'd resented being pulled into the family business. But Rachel had seen just how good he was at not only handling the day-to-day running of the magazine but at dealing with people and managing disasters. She'd eventually convinced him that he was meant to run this business.

And he'd really come into his own over the last

several months—ever since his father, Patrick, had kicked off a competition among his children.

Old man Elliott had determined that the best way to name a new CEO of Elliott Publication Holdings was to see who was willing to work hardest to earn it. At the end of the year the editor in chief of whichever one of the magazines showed the most proportional profit growth would become Top Dog.

And *The Buzz* was the front-runner.

Shane's father was due to announce the winner any day now.

Patrick was a sneaky old man, in Rachel's opinion. Nice, sure, but sneaky. He'd found a way to make his grown children admit just how much they wanted to succeed. By pitting them against each other, he'd been able to sit back all year and watch them discover themselves.

And there had been plenty of discoveries, she thought, remembering all of the turmoil over the last year.

"Did you put that call in to Fin for me?" Shane asked, breathing hard as he picked up the pace on the treadmill.

"Yes," Rachel said, flipping back a page in her memo book. Smiling, she read off, "Fin says and I quote, 'Tell Shane he needs to get away from the city and smell some fresh air. Come to Colorado and I'll teach him to ride a horse.'"

Shane laughed. "A month on a ranch and she's Annie Oakley?"

Rachel chuckled along with him. She couldn't

help it. Shane's twin sister had been sad for so long, it was good knowing that she was finally happy. She'd reconciled with Jessie, the daughter she was forced to give up for adoption so many years ago. She was married to a man she was clearly nuts about and her newly discovered pregnancy was the icing on the cake. "She's happy."

"Yeah," Shane said, his running steps slowing a little as he thought about the sister he was so close to. "She really is. But damn, I miss having her around."

His eyes narrowed thoughtfully as he stared straight ahead, out the bank of windows overlooking Park Avenue.

"I know," Rachel said. "But she'll probably come back home for Christmas."

"Christmas." He shut off the treadmill, stepped neatly to one side and used his towel to wipe his face again. "It's December, isn't it?"

"All month," she agreed.

"Have I started shopping yet?"

"No."

"Damn." Grabbing the second bottle of water, he chugged down the liquid, then handed off the empty bottle. "No time to worry about it now, though. I'm gonna grab a shower, then I'll see you back in the office in half an hour. I'd like to take a look at the new copy for the magazine before it heads out to production."

"Right." Rachel winced as she thought about one column in particular that he'd be going over.

As if reading her mind, he turned and called back, "The new Tess Tells All column was turned in on time, right?"

"Oh, yeah. She's very dependable."

From across the room, Shane winked at her. "Just like you, Rachel."

She watched him disappear into the men's locker room and as the door swung shut behind him, she whispered, "You have *no* idea."

A few hours later, Shane listened with half an ear as his art director, Jonathon Taylor, laid out plans for next summer's Fourth of July edition even as snow flurries dusted the windows. On a weekly magazine, they usually operated months in advance. And the specialty editions required even more in-depth planning.

Jonathon really thrived on the rush of trying to outdo himself with every holiday issue. And damned if he didn't pull it off most of the time. Right now Jon was in the midst of describing, with wildly waving hands, his salute to patriotism, centering on celebrities dressed in red, white and blue. Not original, but knowing Jon, it would be great.

Sandy Hall, the managing editor, was practically frothing at the mouth. No doubt she had a complaint or two about the money Jonathon was budgeting for his blowout edition.

And Shane would have to listen to both sides and make a decision. Used to be that he hated being here, listening to all of the day-to-day drama of the magazine's inner circles. Now, though, he was enjoying himself.

Amazed him to admit it, but there it was. He'd been getting a charge out of running *The Buzz* for months now. Surprisingly enough, Shane realized he was pleased. Proud, even, of how well *The Buzz* was doing. He'd gone into this contest with halfhearted enthusiasm. But as the months had worn on, Shane had found himself being swept up into the competitive spirit. Nothing an Elliott liked better than a contest.

"So—" Jonathon was wrapping up his speech "—I figure if we shell out top dollar to a few of the biggest celebrities, the rest of 'em will come along, too. Nobody wants to feel left out."

Before Shane could respond, Sandy stood up, brushed her short blond hair back from her eyes and narrowed her gaze on Jon. "And if we pay top dollar for a handful of celebs, who's going to offset that expenditure?"

"You have to pay to play," Jon said smugly, shooting a glance at Shane as if knowing he'd back him up.

And he did. "Jon's right, Sandy," he said, holding up one hand to keep his managing editor's temper in check. "We get the right people into that issue, the advertisers will line up to be a part of it. Plus, we'll sell more copies."

"The budget's already stretched pretty thin, Shane," Sandy said, sneering at Jon's gleeful chortle.

"Bull." Shane stood up behind his desk, swept the

edges of his jacket back and stuffed his hands into his pockets. "You know as well as I do that the profit margins are way up. We're beating the pants off the rest of the Elliott magazines. And we're going to keep doing it. And the way we're going to keep doing it is by *not* cutting corners."

Jon slapped one hand to his chest and bowed his head as if in prayer. "Brilliant, my king, brilliant."

Shane laughed at the dramatics, but hey, it was good to be king.

"You're only saying that because you won," Sandy pointed out.

"Sure," Jon said, grinning at her now that he'd made his point.

"Before the bloodletting starts up again," Shane interrupted, looking from one editor to the other, "has either of you made any headway on the job I gave you?"

Jon and Sandy looked at each other, shrugged, then turned back to Shane.

"Nope." Sandy spoke first, clearly reluctant to admit that she'd failed. "I've talked to everyone I know and *nobody* has a clue about this woman's identity."

"I second that," Jon said, obviously disappointed. "Our little Tess is like Spider-Man or something, keeping her secret identity so secret, there's not even a whisper of gossip about her."

Just what Shane hadn't wanted to hear. Damn it. Tess Tells All was the most popular column in his magazine. They'd picked up thousands of new readers thanks to the anonymous woman's talent for being both funny and insightful.

Seven months ago *The Buzz* had carried the very first of the mystery woman's columns.

The response had been immediate. Calls, e-mails, letters, all from people who wanted to read more from Tess. But the woman was untraceable. She faxed her monthly column in from a different location in the city every time and her checks were sent to a PO box and then forwarded to yet another.

As well as *The Buzz* was doing, Shane knew it would be doing even better if he could just talk this woman into writing a weekly column. But she hadn't answered any letters he'd sent and all other attempts at communication had failed.

Making him one very frustrated man.

"Fine," he said on a sigh. "Never mind. Just keep looking for her." Then he sat down behind his desk, waved one hand at them dismissively and picked up the latest column by the mysterious Tess. He didn't even look up when his co-workers left his office.

He read every issue of *The Buzz* before it was laid out for production and eventual printing. The only way to keep a handle on what his magazine was doing was for him to stay involved. From the ground up.

But reading this particular column was always a pleasure. He leaned back in the black leather chair and swung around until he was facing the snow-dusted bank of windows overlooking Manhattan. He smiled ruefully as he read.

Tess says, the secret to surviving your boss is to never let him know you understand him. The poor guy's got to have a few illusions.

My boss thinks he's mysterious. Right. About as mysterious as a pot of chicken soup. The man, like all others of his gender, is so very predictable.

Just last week, I set up two "first dates" for him. At the same restaurant, with the same meal, the same wine. Only the names of the women were changed. Mysterious? Hardly.

I juggle his women just like I juggle his business meetings. The man has made me a good enough juggler that I could be making twice as much money working at a circus— and hey, the co-workers wouldn't change that much!

Shane chuckled. Tess was good, but he felt sorry for her. Working for a man like that couldn't be easy.

When it comes to business, though, he's at the top of his game when everything around him is falling to pieces. Which, I suppose, is why I'm still here after all this time. Despite having to run the man's social life, I do enjoy being at the top. I like being the right hand woman—even if sometimes I feel invisible.

Invisible? Shane shook his head. How could a woman like Tess go unnoticed by anyone?

Maybe it's the time of year that's got me thinking about my life. Sure, you're reading this column sometime in March, but as I write this, it's December. Snow's falling outside, turning Manhattan into a postcard. Wreaths are up on the shop windows, twinkling lights are everywhere and people are ice skating in Rockefeller Center.

The old year is winding down and a new one's getting ready to roll. And I have to ask myself if I really want to maintain the status quo. Is this all there is? Do I really want to keep working for a man who treats me like a well-trained dog? Toss me a treat every now and then so I'll keep running and fetching?

He frowned, wondering why the tone of Tess's column had suddenly changed. Usually she was funny, lighthearted. Making jokes about her boss and underlining, apparently, how every other assistant in the country felt about his or her job.

When he read the next line, he sat up straight in his chair and scowled at the page.

Wonder what he'd do if I quit?

Quit?

She couldn't quit. Hell, her column was too damn popular for her to quit working. If she walked away from her job, she wouldn't be writing this column anymore and where did that leave *The Buzz*?

The truth is, my boss probably wouldn't even notice I was gone until his dry cleaning went unclaimed or until he had to make his own reservations for dinner with the latest wide-eyed blonde. So why'm I still here?

I think we all know the answer to that.

I've let him become too important to me.

I spend more time living his life than I do living my own.

Shane really didn't like the sound of this.

What do you readers think? Should I give it up and stop torturing myself? Should I finally realize that he's never going to look up and notice me? The real me? Should I accept that all I'll ever be to him is an excellent assistant?

Shane grumbled and finished reading the column with a snarl on his face.

The answer to that question is no. The time has come to leave my job and move on to something else while I still can. To all of you assistants out there—all of you who've written to me over the last several months, telling me your own stories—I guess this is goodbye.

Goodbye?

By the time you read this, I'll probably be long gone. I'll miss you guys. I'll miss this column. Heck, I'll miss the boss, too.

I wish you all the best of luck with your own bosses and I'll never forget any of you.

Two

Shane hit the intercom button and when Rachel answered a second later, he snapped, "Come in here for a minute, please."

A moment later the double doors opened and Rachel stepped in, carrying a steno pad. "What's up?"

"Did you see the Tess Tells All column for March?"

"Yeeesss..." One word came out in four distinct syllables.

"So you know she's thinking about quitting her job?"

Rachel took a deep breath and turned her back on him for a second. Deliberately she schooled her features into a politely interested mask. Deciding to quit her job hadn't been an easily reached decision, but she knew it was the right one. Asking her readers for their votes had merely been a way of breaking the news about that decision.

Quietly she shut the door then walked across the thick red carpet toward his desk. "I read it. What's the problem?"

"The problem?" Shane dropped Tess's column onto his desktop and stood up. "She's too popular with our readers, that's the problem. She can't quit her job. We need her column."

Rachel wondered if Shane would be this concerned when she turned in her resignation. And if he were, would that change her mind? No. She had to leave EPH. Had to get out into the world and find someone else to care for. Hopefully someone who would care for her in return.

She shook her head as she sat down in the black leather armchair opposite his desk. Taking another deep breath, she steadied her voice. "I doubt this is a whim. She's obviously done a lot of thinking. Probably some soul searching. People don't just walk away from a good job without a lot of thought."

Which she knew for a fact, since she'd spent the last five months talking herself into doing just that.

He narrowed his gaze on her. "Do you know something you're not telling me?"

"Why would you think that?" Oh, good one, she told herself. Stall without actually lying.

She blew out a breath and tucked a loose strand

of honey-blond hair behind her right ear. She worried her bottom lip and said, "Honestly, Shane, I don't see how you're going to keep her from quitting her job when you don't even know who she is."

"We have to find out."

Rachel tucked her pad against her chest and folded her arms over it. "Haven't you had people working on that for months now?"

"Yes," he muttered, then turned toward the bank of windows. Staring down at the snow-covered street eighteen floors below, he added, "I can't understand how she can stay so hidden. Hell, you'd think her *boss* would recognize himself in her articles."

Rachel mmm-hmmed. "You would, wouldn't you?"

"How could he not?" Shane wondered, more to himself than to her.

"It's surprising, all right," Rachel said dryly. She knew darn well Shane had read every one of the articles she'd written as Tess. And yet, here he stood, completely clueless.

He glanced at her and Rachel caught the glint in his clear green eyes and recognized it. He'd had the same look in his eyes when this competition with his brothers and sisters was just getting started. Shane Elliott simply did *not* lose well. But this time, he was going to have to deal with it.

"Do you know something about Tess you haven't told me?"

She paused just a fraction of a second, then shook her head firmly again even as she skipped around his question. "She faxes those columns in from all over the city. No one knows where the next one's coming from."

He stared at her for a minute or two longer. Long enough to worry Rachel just a little. Good thing he couldn't read her mind. Although, if he *could* read her mind, she wouldn't have to quit her job, because he'd *know* that she loved him and then he'd either be pleased about it or fire her.

"Right," Shane said. "Right." Walking back to his desk, he slid Tess's column into the manila envelope with the rest of the layout for the March issue. Handing it to her, he said, "Get these to production for me, will you, Rachel?"

"Sure." Glad to be on safer ground, she asked, "Anything else?"

He dropped into his chair, braced both arms on his desk and said, "Just find the mysterious Tess. If she's looking for a new job, we'll give her one."

Rachel turned and left the office and when she'd closed the door behind her, she leaned back against it. Hah. Shane wanted to offer Tess a job? Ironic? Oh, yeah.

She walked past her desk and on down the hall toward production. She glanced to either side of her as her heels sank deeply into the rich scarlet carpet. It was going to be hard to leave this place. It was familiar. Comfortable.

Maybe *too* comfortable, she reminded herself.

The gleaming glass and chrome offices on either side of the wide aisle were bustling with sound as the staff of *The Buzz* worked on various tasks. Phones rang, someone laughed and the scent of coffee floated on the warm air drifting from the central heating system.

Rachel smiled at Stacy, the receptionist, as she strolled through the main waiting area. The walls were a clean, pure white, and the art on the walls mostly enlarged, chrome-framed covers of *The Buzz*. The effect was startling, but eye catching. The idea was to make this floor look up to the minute, fresh. Exciting. And it worked.

Every floor of the EPH building had its own color scheme and was decorated according to whichever magazine it was trying to promote. Rachel was probably prejudiced, but she'd always thought the eighteenth-floor home of *The Buzz* was the nicest.

Rachel kept walking, tossing a glance into the small meeting rooms as she walked, smiling in at one or two of the people she passed. The photography lab door was closed and she smiled wryly. Ferria—no last name—was notoriously territorial about her office. Even Shane had a hard time getting past the lead photographer's doorway.

At Production, Rachel stepped through the open door and handed over the manila envelope to the head man's assistant, Christina. Fiftyish, Christina was a single mother of four boys who took no crapola off of anyone—least of all her boss. Her snow-white hair was cut into extremely short layers that hugged her head and highlighted bright blue eyes.

The older woman pushed her silver wire-framed glasses up on her nose and grinned. "I'm thinking about heading out to Lucci's Deli for lunch. Want to join me?"

"Love it," Rachel said, realizing that Christina was only one of so many people she'd miss when she left. "I'll meet you at the elevator at twelve, okay?"

"Excellent."

Walking back to her desk, she felt almost as though she were already saying goodbye. Her gaze swept over the familiar fixtures and faces and she hugged the electrical hum of activity close. She was really going to miss this place.

She loved her job. Loved working for Shane and feeling as though she were a part of something special. Working on a weekly magazine, there was always something happening. An air of excitement, urgency that she would probably never find anywhere else.

But she knew she had to go.

She couldn't stay at *The Buzz*, working with Shane every day, loving him as she did. It was just too hard. Too hard to make his dates for him, to see him look at every other woman in the world with more interest than he would ever show her. So whether she liked it or not, it was time, Rachel thought, that she left EPH.

Both she and her alter ego Tess were going to quietly disappear from Shane's life.

And there was nothing he could do to change her mind.

By seven o'clock, most of the magazine's employees were gone. Shane walked through the empty office and listened to the sound of his own footsteps on the carpet. Only a few of the overhead lights were on, splashing the shadows with occasional bursts of light. The reflected lights shone against the black expanse of windows and mirrored Shane as he walked toward the elevator.

During the day, this office thundered with the noise of productivity. People laughing, talking, computer keys clicking, phones ringing. But at night…it was like a house emptied of its children.

Quiet to the point of spooky.

He passed reception, where an acre of desk sat dead center of a waiting area. Twin couches in matching shades of white faced each other across the expanse and on the far wall, the elevator gleamed dully in the overhead light.

Sighing, Shane stabbed the up call button and waited impatiently for the elevator to arrive. If he hadn't answered that phone call from his father a few minutes ago, he'd have been pushing the down button and heading for home to get ready for his date with… He frowned. What the *hell* was that woman's name?

Shaking his head, he pushed that question away to concentrate on another one. Why did his father want to see him? And why now, after the business day?

Patrick Elliott was a hard man. Always had been. More focused on building an empire than a family, over the years he'd become a stranger to his own children. Shane's mother, Maeve, was the glue that held the Elliott family together. Hell, *she* was the only reason he and his siblings were still speaking to Patrick.

The elevator opened in front of him and he stepped inside with all the enthusiasm of a man heading to a tax audit. Generic Muzak filtered down all around him, but he did his best to ignore it. He punched the appropriate floor button, and as the doors slid shut again, Shane let his mind drift back over the years.

In all the memories he had of growing up, Patrick was no more than a blurred image on the fringes of his mind. Until one memorable year.

He and his twin, Finola, were the youngest of the Elliott children. And, since they'd been born nine years after their brother Daniel, Shane and Fin were even closer than twins usually were. Growing up, they'd been each other's best friend. They'd fought each other's battles, celebrated each other's victories, and shared the hurts and pains that came along.

And maybe, Shane told himself, that was the main reason he just couldn't bring himself to get close to his father now. Patrick was trying to make up for his failures as a parent and slowly, each of the Elliott kids was coming around. But Shane held back—because he'd never been able to forgive the old man for what he'd put Fin through when she was just a kid.

He leaned back against the cool, slick chrome of the elevator wall and closed his eyes, remembering. Shane could see Fin as she'd been at fifteen, beautiful, trusting, with bright green eyes filled with anticipation. Until she'd made the mistake that Patrick wouldn't countenance.

She'd become pregnant by the son of another wealthy family, and neither side wanted their children getting married for the sake of a child they hadn't planned.

Though their mother had cried and sided with Fin—something none of the children knew until recently—Patrick had been adamant about saving the family's "good name." He'd shipped Fin off to a convent in Canada with as much feeling as a man who dropped off an unwanted puppy at the pound. No one had been able to reach Patrick. The old man never backed down from a damn thing if he believed he was right—and he *always* believed he was right.

Fin was forced to give up her daughter at birth and Shane would never be able to forget her pain, her misery. Just as he was pretty sure he'd never be able to completely forgive Patrick for causing it.

The elevator dinged as it reached the executive level of the EPH building and the doors slid open with a whoosh.

"Might as well get this over with," Shane muttered and walked into a very different atmosphere than the one found on the eighteenth floor. On the twenty-third, the carpeting was subdued, the walls a soft beige with cream trim and the furniture was elegant antiques. Even the air smelled different up here, he thought, more…rarified, he supposed.

But then, that's what Patrick had always been concerned about. How things looked. The perception of the Elliott family. Which was why it had taken Fin too many years to reconnect with her long lost daughter.

At least *that* had come around and turned out well. Now that Jessie was finally where she'd always belonged—with them—Patrick had at last accepted and welcomed the girl. And the pain Shane had seen in Fin's eyes for too many years was finally gone.

Knowing Fin was so happy had made dealing with Patrick easier than it used to be.

Shaking his head, he wondered where all the philosophical thoughts were coming from. Hell, he was wasting time. He still had to get home and change for his date with…what was her name?

Grumbling, he knocked briefly on the closed door to Patrick's office and waited.

"Come on in."

Opening the door, he stepped into an elegantly appointed office and looked directly at his father, seated behind a mahogany desk fit for a king.

At seventy-seven, Patrick Elliott looked at least ten years younger than his age. Still had most of his hair, though it was completely gray now. Tall, with squared shoulders and a defiant tilt to his chin, the old man continued to look like he'd be able to take on the world, if necessary.

Shane walked across the office and dropped into a burgundy leather club chair opposite his father's desk. Absently he noted that the chair was built to be lower than Patrick's desk, leaving whoever sat in it at a disadvantage. That was his father, though. Never miss a trick. "What can I do for you, Dad?"

Patrick leaned back in his chair, braced his elbows on the padded arms and steepled his fingers. "In a hurry, are you?"

"Not really." Of course he was, but if he admitted as much, Patrick was contrary enough to slow this meeting down. Crossing his legs, Shane rested his right ankle on his left knee and idly tapped his fingers against the soft leather of his shoe.

Nodding, the old man said, "That's all right. I am in a hurry. Your mother's got us tickets to some play or other."

Shane smiled. "A musical?"

Patrick shuddered. "Probably."

This time Shane dipped his head to hide a broader smile. His parents were sharply divided on the theater. His father hated it and his mother loved it. One thing he could give Patrick Elliott. The man was crazy enough about his wife that he'd actually suffered through seeing *Cats* twelve times.

"God knows what she's gonna make me endure tonight. But she's meeting me here in twenty minutes, so I'm gonna make this short."

"All right." Back to business, then. "Let's hear it."

Patrick leaned forward in his chair and gave his son

a broad smile. "The final reports are in. All of the profit margins on each of the magazines has been tallied."

"And...?" Shane's heartbeat quickened and a sense of expectation filled him. Hell, just a year ago, if someone had told him he'd care this much about being named CEO of Elliot Publication Holdings, he would have laughed himself sick.

Now?

Hell, he wanted that position more than he cared to admit. And even more, he wanted to *win* the competition his father had instigated.

"Congratulations," Patrick said.

Shane let out a breath he hadn't realized he'd been holding. "Yeah?" He grinned and stood up. "Thanks."

The old man stood, too, and held out one hand. Shane grabbed it and gave it a shake.

"You did a good job, son."

A surprising zip of pleasure shot through Shane. Apparently, he thought wryly, no one outgrew the need for approval from a parent. Even one who'd been as absent from his children's lives as Patrick.

"Appreciate it," Shane said, reeling in his thoughts as they careened wildly through his mind. CEO. It meant a world of responsibilities that only a year or so ago he would have done anything he could to avoid. Weird how a man's life could change.

He couldn't wait to tell Rachel. All the work they'd been doing for the last few years had finally culminated in winning the grand prize.

"I'll make the official announcement at the family

New Year's party," Patrick was saying as he came around the edge of his desk. "But I wanted you to know now. You earned it, Shane."

"Damn straight I did," Shane said, still feeling the hum of excitement. Gratification. "But I couldn't have done it without my staff. The people at *The Buzz* have worked their asses off this last year. Especially Rachel, my assistant."

The older man nodded, pleased. "I'm glad you realize that no man succeeds alone."

Shane slanted his father a look. "Oh, I know it. I'm just sort of surprised that *you* know it."

Patrick sighed and shook his head. "A man reaches a certain age and he gets to know all sorts of things, Shane. Things he should have realized a long time ago."

"Yeah, well," Shane said, suddenly uncomfortable. "Better late than never, I guess."

"I suppose. At the first of the year, I'll clear my stuff out of this office and you can move in."

"Seems strange. Thinking about me, working up here."

"Seems damn strange to me, too, son," Patrick said, wandering across the room to stare at the plaques and framed awards EPH had won over the years. "I'm so used to coming here every day," he murmured, "I can't really imagine *not* working."

"Hell, I can't even remember the last time you took a vacation."

The older man glanced over his shoulder at Shane. His eyes flashed with something that might have been regret, but it was gone so fast, Shane couldn't be sure. And even if it was regret, he told himself, what did it change?

"I made mistakes," Patrick admitted, turning around now to face his son. "I know that."

Shane stiffened slightly. He didn't want to head down Memory Lane with his father. Especially since those memories would no doubt douse the feeling of victory still rushing through him. Over the last year, Patrick had made a sincere effort to get to know his children. But the bottom line was, one good year didn't offset a lifetime. "Dad—"

"I know. You don't want to talk about it. Well, neither do I." Shoving both hands into the pockets of his well-tailored dark blue suit, the older man said, "But I can't help thinking about it. I can't rewrite the past, though I wish to hell I could. All those years, I focused on my work. Building a legacy for you and your brothers and sisters."

"And you did it."

"Yes, I did. But along the way," he said, his voice suddenly sounding tired, "I missed what was really important. It all slipped out of my reach and I let it go. Did it to myself. No one else to blame."

"There doesn't have to be blame," Shane said quietly. "Not anymore."

"Wish I believed that," Patrick whispered and he suddenly looked every one of his seventy-seven years. "But the mistakes I made are the point of this conversation."

"Meaning?"

"Meaning don't do what I did." He pulled his hands from his pockets and waved his arms to encompass the high-rise office, the awards and the incredible view from the bank of floor to ceiling windows behind his desk. "Right now, being in charge looks great. The challenge. The fun of beating the others."

Shane shrugged.

"I know you, son," Patrick said, stabbing his index finger at Shane. "I know you thrive on the competition, just like a true Elliott. But remember, winning doesn't mean a damn thing if you've got nothing but the victory to show for it."

Three

Rachel opened the freezer door for the third time in a half hour and stared at her nemesis. It sat there next to a stack of frozen dinners and mocked her silently.

Her own fault. She never should have bought it. But she'd had a weak moment right after work.

Well, actually, she'd been having plenty of weak moments lately. Every time she thought about quitting her job and walking away from her only connection to Shane Elliott.

"It's the right thing to do," she muttered as icy fog wafted from the freezer to caress her face.

Her hand tightened on the white plastic door handle and she squeezed as if gripping a lifeline. She had to quit. She knew it. She'd only been postponing the inevitable because she hadn't wanted to leave EPH until Shane had won the competition between him and his siblings.

"Well, that excuse is gone. You've helped *The Buzz* do so well in this last year that he's *bound* to win. What've you got left?" she asked herself, knowing damn well there wasn't an answer.

She shivered, and reached into the freezer, her fingers curling around a small carton covered in ice crystals. "Fine. I surrender. We both knew I would or I wouldn't have bought you in the first place."

When a knock sounded on her front door, she backed up instantly, leaving the carton where it was and slammed the freezer shut. She ran both hands over her wavy blond hair, released from the tidy French twist she kept it in while working. Then she automatically smoothed the gray skirt she still wore and shuffled out of the tiny galley kitchen in her pink fuzzy slippers. As she walked, she glanced at the pineapple shaped clock on the wall.

Eight o'clock.

Great.

Shane would be just sitting down to his first glass of champagne with Tawny the wonder girl. Glad she'd reminded herself of *that*. Oh, yeah, it was definitely time to quit her job.

She passed her overstuffed sofa on the way to the door and absently straightened a bright blue throw pillow. Rachel's gaze flicked quickly around her West Village apartment in approval. Only a one bedroom, it was plenty big enough for her. Plus, it was a family neighborhood, with a deli on one corner and a small grocery store on another.

In the five years she'd lived here, she'd transformed the old apartment into a cozy nest. She'd painted the walls a soft, French country lemon-yellow and done the trim in pale off-white. The furniture was large, overstuffed and covered in a floral fabric that made her feel as if she lived in a garden.

Natalie Cole sang to her from the stereo on the far wall and from downstairs, came the tempting scent of her neighbor Mrs. Florio's homemade lasagna. With any luck, Rachel thought, scuffing her slippers over the hardwood floor, she'd be getting a care basket of leftovers in the morning. Mrs. Florio, God bless her, thought Rachel was far too skinny to "catch a nice man" and took every opportunity to fatten her up.

Smiling to herself, Rachel looked through the security peephole and sucked in a gasp as she jumped back, startled.

Shane?

Here?

He knocked again.

She took another peek and watched as he leaned in toward the fisheye lens and grinned. "Rachel, come on. Open up."

Quickly she gave herself a once-over. Still in the yellow silk blouse and gray skirt she'd worn to work, she suddenly wished she was dressed in sequins and rhinestones and on her way out the door to meet…*anybody*.

"How do you know I'm here?" she demanded. "I could be out on a hot date." Sure. In an alternate universe.

"You're talking to me," he said, still grinning into the peephole. "So you're there. Now, you going to let me in or what?"

In the four years she'd worked for Shane he'd never once come to her apartment. So what in heaven would bring him here now? Did he somehow sense she was going to quit? Was he trying to undermine her decision?

"This is so not fair," she muttered as she quickly undid the chain, then twisted first one, then another dead bolt locks. Finally she turned the knob and opened the door.

Shane didn't wait for an invitation; he crowded past her into the living room, then turned around to look at her. In one hand, he held a bouquet of lilacs—Rachel's favorite flower—and in the other a huge bottle of champagne.

Stomach jittering, Rachel closed the door and leaned back against it. "What're you doing here, Shane?"

"This is a nice place," he said, glancing around at the apartment.

"Thanks."

"Wasn't easy to find," he added. "Had to go down to personnel and look up your records to get your address."

Her stomach did another wild twist and flip and she swallowed hard. "And why would you do that?"

"So I could bring you these," he said, handing her the lilacs.

The heavy, sweet perfume reached for her and Rachel just managed to keep from burying her nose in the blossoms and enjoying the thrill of Shane bringing her flowers. But there was something else going on here and she had to know what it was.

"Shane, why are you bringing me flowers?" she asked, silently congratulating herself on the steadiness of her voice. "Aren't you supposed to be at Une Nuit giving Tawny a bouquet of daisies?"

"Tawny!" He slapped the heel of his hand against his forehead. *"That's* her name. Why can't I remember that?"

"Good question," Rachel said. "Maybe because there are too many Tawnys, Bambis and Barbies in your life to keep them straight?"

He slanted her a look and then smiled and shrugged. "Maybe." Sweeping his gaze around the room again, he started for the kitchen, talking over his shoulder as he went. "Anyway, don't worry about what's her name. I called Stash. Told him I couldn't make it and to give…"

"Tawny," Rachel provided as she followed him into her kitchen.

"…right. Told him to give Tawny whatever she wanted on the house and to offer my apologies."

"So you stood her up."

"Had to," he said, setting the champagne bottle down onto the counter and shifting a look at the white cupboards. "Champagne glasses?"

Still clutching her lilacs, Rachel pointed with her free hand. "Just wineglasses, sorry."

He shrugged again. "That's fine." Then he opened the cupboard door, reached two glasses and set them on the counter.

This was too hard. Now that she'd seen him here, in her place, she'd never really be able to get him out again. She'd always be able to pull up the memory of him standing in her living room, rooting through her kitchen. Heck, she'd probably never be able to look through the peephole again without seeing his smiling face looking back at her.

"You shouldn't be here," she blurted, fingers tightening around the lilacs that must have cost him a small fortune.

Springtime flowers in the dead of winter? And she was sappy enough to really enjoy knowing that he'd remembered *her* favorite flowers even when he couldn't remember Tawny's.

His fingers on the wire cage of the bottle top, he paused to glance at her. His gaze swept her up and down, from her tousled hair to the tips of her furry slippers. Slowly a smile curved his mouth. "Why? You really do have a hot date?"

Straightening up a little, she said, "I was planning on spending the night with *two* guys, actually."

"Yeah? Who?"

Rachel sighed. It was pointless to pretend, since she wasn't exactly dressed for going clubbing. "Ben and Jerry."

Shane grinned as he started working on the champagne cork again. "This'll be better."

"I don't know," she said, moving past him to grab a cut glass vase from another cupboard. She glanced at him as she filled the vase with water. "It's *chocolate* ice cream."

"Not nearly good enough for the occasion."

"Which is?" she asked, stuffing the lilacs into the vase and giving them one last, lingering caress.

"We're celebrating." The cork popped, slamming into a cupboard before bouncing to the floor, and Shane held the bottle over the sink as champagne frothed and foamed out the neck. As he filled both of the heavy green glasses to the rim, he looked down at her, winked and teased, "Ask me what we're celebrating."

A jolt of excitement sizzled inside her. "What're we celebrating?"

"We did it, Rachel," he said, setting the bottle down and handing her one of the glasses. He picked up his own then clinked it against hers. "We won the contest. I'm the new CEO."

That single jolt of excitement burst into a fireworks display of pleasure that lit up her insides like the Fourth of July. "Shane, that's great."

It was. It really was. Even though it was now official and Rachel knew she'd be leaving, she was just so damn happy for him. He'd worked hard for this and really deserved it. That he was so pleased about it only went to show how much he'd changed in the last few years.

"I know," he said, taking her elbow and leading her out of the kitchen into the living room. He steered her onto the couch, said, "I'll be right back," and went back to the kitchen to retrieve the champagne.

He set the bottle down on the glass-topped coffee table, then sat down beside Rachel on the sofa. She watched him over the rim of her glass while she took a huge swallow. Bubbles filled her nose, her mouth and apparently, her mind.

Watching him, Rachel wanted to reach out and smooth back the lock of dark hair lying across his forehead. She curled her fingers around the stem of her glass to keep from doing just that. Instead she settled for looking at him. Shane had always been a good stare. The man was simply gorgeous.

Shining moss-green eyes, strong chin, wide smile and broad shoulders. He was the stuff that dreams were made of. Rachel should know. He filled her dreams almost nightly.

"You know," he was saying, "when my father broke the news to me a while ago, all I could think about was that you should have been there to hear it, too."

She took another gulp of champagne, hoping to ease the sudden dryness in her throat.

"You're the real reason I won, Rachel."

A happy little glow dazzled her insides, but she deliberately squashed it. "That's not true, Shane. You worked hard for this. You deserve it."

"Maybe," he said nodding, running the tip of his

index finger around the rim of his glass. "But even if it's true, I couldn't have done it without you."

"Oh, absolutely," she agreed smiling.

So much easier to keep this conversation light and teasing, as she always did. So much better for her equilibrium if she didn't start fantasizing about Shane throwing himself at her feet, proclaiming his love and begging her to marry him.

Oh for heaven's sake.

She took another big drink of champagne and didn't complain when Shane reached for the bottle and topped off her glass and then his own.

"We'll be moving into my father's office at the first of the year."

You will, she thought silently, wishing she could stay. Wishing she could be a part of his life. But it was just getting too painful.

"I'm guessing you'll want to redecorate," she said wryly.

"Oh, yeah." His grin was devastating. All the more so since he seemed to be oblivious to the power he wielded. "I can't stand the antique thing, but the glass and chrome look doesn't seem right for up there, either."

"I guess not," she said, as the music playing shifted from a drum pounding dance rhythm to something slow and sultry.

"This means a big raise," Shane said, leaning back into the sofa cushion. "For both of us."

"Uh-huh." A raise would have been nice.

"And a bonus," he said, "if you can locate our

mysterious columnist and convince her to keep writing for *The Buzz*."

"Shane—"

"I know," he interrupted, "we haven't been able to find her, but she's out there somewhere, Rachel."

"And doesn't want to be found." Oh, she really didn't want to be found.

"Yeah, but I've been thinking," he said, refilling their glasses again.

Rachel looked at the bubbles in her wineglass and told herself to stop drinking it so quickly. Already, her mind was a little fuzzy and her vision blurred just a little bit. Should have eaten that ice cream, she told herself.

She shook her head and told herself to pay attention as Shane kept talking.

"Tess said she's quitting her job. So I'm thinking, what if we just hire her to work for us?"

"She does," Rachel argued and wondered why her tongue suddenly felt a little thick. "She writes a column for *The Buzz*."

"Yeah, but if we made her a *staff* writer, she could call her own shots. Do advice, gossip, whatever." He jumped to his feet as if unable to sit still beneath the onslaught of too many ideas. "The readers love her, Rachel. She's funny and smart and that comes across in her column."

She almost said thank you. Catching herself just in time, Rachel frowned at her champagne and leaned forward to carefully set her glass on the coffee table. A buzz was good. Drunk was not.

"Why is this so important to you, Shane?"

He turned around to look at her. Taking a long gulp of his wine, he shook his head. "Not sure. All I know is she's good and I'm not going to let her slip away."

"I don't think you have much choice."

He smiled at her and something warm and liquid slid through her veins, leaving a trail of fire that seemed to be burning right through her skin.

Oh, boy.

"That's where you're wrong. You're my secret weapon, Rachel."

"Me?"

"You've got more contacts in the city than the mayor. You can find out who Tess is and where we can find her."

"Oh, I don't think so."

Setting his glass down on the table, Shane reached for her and pulled her to her feet. She swayed a little, but he steadied her fast.

"Rachel, you can't quit on me now."

Quit? How'd he know she was going to quit? She stared up at him and, just for a minute or two, lost herself in the green of his eyes. "Did you know," she whispered, "you have tiny gold flakes in your eyes?"

The smile faded from his face and his hands on her arms gentled, his thumbs rubbing against her silk blouse. "I do?"

"Yes," she said, leaning in even closer, tipping her head back to keep her gaze locked with his. "I never really noticed before, but…"

"Your eyes are green, too," he said, his voice

almost lost under the slow pulse of the music. "Soft green. Like summer grass."

Her pulse quickened, her heartbeat jangled wildly and a swirl of something hot and needy settled in the pit of her stomach. And Rachel was loving every minute of it.

His hands slid across her back and dropped to her waist. She felt the heat of his touch right through the fabric of her blouse and she wondered absently if his handprints were branded on her skin.

She hoped so.

"Rachel," he whispered, his hands moving on her back again in long, languorous strokes that fanned the fire simmering inside her into hungry flames. He took a breath, held it as his gaze moved over her face as if he'd never seen her before. As if she were the most beautiful thing on the planet. Then he released that pent-up breath and said, "I'd better—"

Go.

He was going to leave.

Already he was releasing her, taking a small step back, putting a small slice of safety between them. And suddenly Rachel knew she couldn't let this moment pass. Let him leave without at least showing him once just how she felt.

"—kiss you," she said, finishing his sentence the way she wanted it to be. She went up on her toes, slid her arms around his neck and tipped her head to one side. He watched her, not moving. She felt the tension in his hands. She was pretty sure time itself stood still for one amazing moment.

Then she laid her mouth over his and put everything she had into the kiss she'd been daydreaming about for a solid year.

Four

For a fraction of a second, Shane was too surprised to react.

He caught up quick.

Rachel's lips were warm and soft and the taste of champagne clung to them, giving him more of a rush than drinking the expensive wine itself had. He pulled her tighter, closer, wrapping his arms around her and squeezing as he devoured her mouth.

Random thoughts flashed through his mind like fireflies winking on and off on a hot summer night.

Rachel.

He was kissing Rachel.

And it felt good.

Right.

Her mouth opened under his tender assault and his tongue swept inside to taste her more deeply. To feel her heat, to claim…something.

Something he couldn't name but knew was within his reach. Something that he'd never thought to find.

Fin had long teased him about the right woman being there under his nose for four years, but he'd never really considered that she might be correct. His twin had hinted that Rachel Adler could, with a little effort on his part, be much more to him than a fabulous assistant.

But he hadn't listened. Hadn't really believed that Rachel and he would be able to…connect so completely. So amazingly.

Her hands slid up his back and he wished to heaven he'd taken his suit jacket off when he arrived. He wanted to feel her small, capable hands with their short, neat nails on his skin.

That thought jolted through him with the impact of a crashing meteor.

Then a ball of fire settled in the pit of his stomach and stretched out tentacles to every corner of his body. Heat radiated from him and fed the raw, raging hunger clawing at his insides.

He tore his mouth from hers and ran his lips down the length of her neck. "Sweet. So sweet."

"Shane." His name, on a sigh of sound that rushed through him with the force of a category 5 hurricane.

Her hands tangled at the back of his neck, fingers twining through his hair, nails scraping his skin.

Sensation boiled within and Shane had to fight for air.

He'd never known such an overwhelming desire. Such a demand from his body.

Such all consuming *need*.

He slipped his hands beneath the tail of her silk shirt and smoothed his palms over her back. Her skin was more tantalizing than the silk. Smoother, softer. He sucked in air like a dying man and licked the pulse point at the base of her throat.

She gasped and tipped her head to one side, silently inviting more of his attention. He gave it to her. As his hands stroked her back, he nibbled at her throat and covered that pounding pulse point until he could taste her need for him throbbing with every beat of her heart.

"Rachel," he murmured against her skin. "I'm not sure what's going on here, but I want you."

"Oh good," she said, sighing again and leaning into him more completely. "That's very good. I want you, too. Now, okay? Does now work for you?"

He smiled and lifted his head to look down into her passion-glazed eyes. His smile faded in a new burst of hunger. "Yeah, now works for me in a big way."

He looked around the room, as if expecting a bed to magically appear. If it didn't, he was thinking the couch would do. Plenty long enough. And if she didn't like the couch, then the floor. Or standing up against a wall.

Something.

Soon.

He had to have her.

Had to bury himself inside her and feel her heat taking him in. Had to watch her eyes blur and feel her breath catch. Had to see a climax shatter the cool green of her eyes.

"Bedroom," she said, lifting one hand to point. "Through there."

"Right." He didn't waste time. Couldn't. Sweeping her up into his arms, he crossed the room in a few long strides and kicked the partially ajar door wide-open.

A double bed with four heavy posts sat against one wall, its mattress covered by a floral quilt. The curtains were open and through the lacy sheers, a streetlight shone from outside, illuminating the softly falling snowflakes drifting past the glass.

They were three stories up. No one was going to be peeking in at them, so Shane left the curtains open to the pale wash of light. He wanted to see her.

Wanted to watch her.

He carried her across the room and set her on her feet. She staggered slightly and Shane smiled. He knew how she felt.

Everything was just a little off center.

"You're not changing your mind, are you?" she asked.

"Not a chance," he whispered and reached for the top button of her blouse. In less than a few seconds he had them all undone and was pushing the silk down her arms to let it fall onto the floor.

"That's good," she said, swallowing hard and nodding. "Really good."

Shane nodded back at her. "How about you? We can still stop."

"Are you kidding?" she asked and stepped into the circle of his arms, wrapping her own arms around his neck and hanging on. She looked up into his eyes and said, "No one leaves this room until we're absolutely through with each other."

He gave her a quick grin. This was the Rachel he knew and admired. Sure of herself. Confident. "I learned a long time ago that it pays to listen to my assistant."

Then he kissed her again and quickly worked the hooks at the back of her bra. The fragile lace parted and she twisted in his arms, freeing herself while simultaneously pushing his jacket off his shoulders.

Shane felt the same urgency pounding inside him and worked with her. In a couple of minutes, they were both naked and tumbling onto the mattress. The quilt was cold against his skin and the fabric felt old and soft. The antique bed creaked and groaned under their combined weight, but neither of them noticed.

In the wash of light streaming through the windows, Shane looked his fill of her. Full breasts, narrow waist and rounded hips—she was built with curves in all the right places, as, in his opinion, all women should be. He ran his hands over those curves, tracing every line with his fingertips until she was writhing beneath him, her breath coming fast and furious.

As her need peaked, so did his. He felt every one of her thundering heartbeats as if it were his own. He touched her and she shivered. He stroked her and she sighed. She lifted one hand to drag her nails across his chest and he felt each gentle scrape as if it were a flaming arrow.

"Yes, yes," she whispered, "you feel so good, Shane." She turned into him, parting her legs for his questing fingers.

His heartbeat jumped, his breath caught. He slid one hand down, down across her rib cage, over her abdomen and past the juncture of her thighs. She jerked in his arms and tried to close her legs.

"Rachel?"

"I'm too on the edge. It's coming. And I don't want it to," she breathed shakily. "I want this to last. I don't want it over so fast."

"It's not over," he assured her, his voice tight, scratching past the knot of need lodged in his throat. "We have all night. Now let me take you."

She clutched at his shoulders as his fingers dipped lower to find her depths. She was hot, damp, ready for his touch. He watched her as he slid his hand lower, caressing her intimate folds.

She gasped and stiffened in his arms at that first molten contact. "Shane!"

Her climax hit her hard, shaking her from head to toe. She tipped her head back into the mattress, bit her bottom lip and, keeping a death grip on his shoulders, shuddered as her body erupted from within.

More aroused than he'd ever been in his life, Shane watched her as she rode the crest of pleasure, shaking, trembling in his grasp, her fingers clutching at him. Mouth dry, pulse hammering, he bent his head and took her mouth as she gasped for air. He wanted to feel that again. Feel her body exploding for him, *because* of him. He wanted to hear her gasp and scream his name.

Her body still shuddering, he took her up again, pushing her high and fast. Sliding first one then two fingers inside her as his thumb stroked the very core of her, he stroked her inside and out.

Rachel dragged in air, knowing it wasn't enough. She might never get enough air again. Her brain was melting, but that was probably because her body was on fire.

The first orgasm had hardly finished shimmering through her when Shane had her on the climb toward number two. And now that she knew how good it was, she couldn't wait for it to happen again. Her body hummed and sizzled. Her blood felt as if it were boiling. Her limbs were weak and energized all at once.

She twisted up closer to him, loving the feel of his skin against hers. The soft curls of dark hair on his chest felt like silk, and the muscles beneath his skin felt like steel. His body was hard and strong and, right at the moment, as necessary to her as the breathing that just wasn't working quite right.

Her mind numbed out, short-circuited from the

onslaught of sensations rocketing through it. She couldn't think, could barely see, and it didn't seem to matter. All that mattered was that he not stop touching her.

His hands moved on her and she opened her legs wider, loving the feel of him on her, *in* her.

He took her mouth again in another kiss and she knew that breathing was no longer an option. But who needed air when she had Shane? His tongue mated with hers in an erotic dance that sent shock waves of need and desire sliding through her system.

His breath brushed her cheek and she moved toward him, somehow trying to burrow into him. She hooked her left leg over his hip and groaned when his fingers dipped deeper inside her.

"I've gotta be in you," he whispered, tearing his mouth from hers to bury his face in the curve of her neck. His whiskers scratched her skin as he licked and tasted his way across her throat and down to her collarbone.

"Oh, yeah, inside me. That's good. That sounds good to me, too."

"Protection," he muttered thickly, dipping his head to bite her neck.

His teeth stroked her fevered skin even as that one word he'd said sailed through her brain and came to a dead stop.

"Protection. Yeah. Okay." And her without a single condom in the house. She couldn't let him leave. Couldn't *not* feel his body within hers. She had to have him. *Now.* Struggling to breathe and think and speak at the same time, Rachel finally found the words she needed. "I'm on the pill. I'm good if you're—"

"Clean as a whistle," he assured her.

"Me, too. Good for us."

"Oh, yeah, excellent for us," he whispered, moving over her, settling himself between her up-drawn thighs. "Best news I've ever heard."

She nodded. "Right there with you."

And then there was no more talking. This was too important for talk. Too important for thought.

Too damn important period.

His body pushed into hers and Rachel's breath caught. She arched up, meeting him, opening for him, welcoming him in deeper, harder. He was so big. So hard.

So wonderful.

He rocked his hips against hers, filling her, engulfing her with sensation. Then he took her hands and, capturing them in his, held them down at either side of her head. She tried to move and couldn't. Then she realized she didn't care about moving. She only wanted to feel.

He stared down into her eyes as he withdrew and advanced, his body lighting hers up like a fireworks show.

Every hard, solid inch of him filled her and when he pulled free of her body only to slide himself home again, Rachel groaned. This was all she'd ever dreamed of, wanted, and more.

As Shane's body drove hers toward completion, she realized that she never could have imagined this. Nothing in her experience—all right, her experience was pretty limited—could have prepared her for this. For the clamoring feelings, the mind-shattering explosions, the frantic, demanding need.

He looked down at her and she stared up into eyes that were green and gold and dark with passion. His generous mouth tight, his jaw locked, he stared into her eyes as if he couldn't have looked away if his life depended on it.

Music poured into the room from the stereo in the living room; the quilt beneath her felt cool and soft. And in the pale light, Rachel burned this image of Shane on her mind so that she would always have it with her.

He kept a tight grip on her hands, pinning her to the bed. Her hips rose and fell with him to the rhythm he set, and when electric sparks began in her bloodstream, she raced with him toward the release she knew was waiting just out of reach.

"Shane?" she called his name aloud. Had to say it. Had to hear it. Had to convince herself that this was real and not just another of her lonely dreams.

"Come for me," he said, his voice a rumble in the dimly lit room. "Come for me again. And then again."

With a shriek of bone-deep ecstasy, she did. Clinging to him as her body exploded into a fiery burst of sparks and color, she was only dimly aware when he called her name and followed her into the void.

A kaleidoscope of colors was still revolving behind her closed eyes when Rachel felt Shane roll off of her and to the edge of the bed. "What?"

She forced her eyes open and looked at him. Just one look was enough to make her body start humming again, ready for another go. Apparently, though, Shane was finished.

"You're *leaving?*"

He looked at her and gave her a grin that weakened her knees enough to make her grateful she was lying down.

"Just going to the living room. For the champagne."

"Ah. Good idea."

"Yeah," he said, leaning down to plant a quick kiss on her mouth. "Seems I'm just full of good ideas tonight."

She watched him leave the room and couldn't complain about the view. He even had a nice butt. But a second later, Rachel closed her eyes again and shifted lazily on the quilt her grandmother had made more than fifty years before. She winced at that thought and rolled off the bed. Quickly she pulled the quilt back and draped it over the foot of the bed, then lay down again on the clean, lavender-scented sheets.

Every inch of her body felt used up and happy.

But just as she acknowledged that fact, her brain started clicking along, demanding to know what she was going to do next. How could she sleep with her boss? How tacky was that? And how could she ever look at him at the office again without imagining that great butt?

Stop it. She didn't want to think.

Not tonight.

Heaven knew there'd be plenty of time for thinking and torturing herself later. For the moment, she only wanted to enjoy what she was feeling.

Icy cold trickled onto her breasts and her eyes flew open.

She looked up, directly into Shane's eyes and her heart thudded in her chest. "What're you…"

He drizzled a little more champagne onto her breasts, then set the bottle down onto the nightstand beside the bed. Climbing in beside her, he said only, "I was thirsty."

Then he bent his head to take first one of her nipples, then the other, into his mouth. His tongue twirled around and around the rigid, sensitive peaks and Rachel groaned as he suckled her. Her fingers curled into the sheet beneath her and she held on tight as her world rocked crazily from side to side.

He lapped at her, nibbled her flesh with the edges of his teeth and then suckled her again. She felt each drawing tug of his mouth straight to the heart of her.

Her body lit up again and when he lifted his head, she wanted to weep for the loss of his mouth. She drew in a deep gulp of air and blew it out again in a rush.

"Still thirsty," he quipped and grabbed the bottle. Carefully, he poured the frothy wine atop her breasts, down her rib cage and let it pool in her belly button.

Rachel shivered, but not because the champagne

was so cold. No, she was only surprised it didn't boil on contact with her skin. "Shane…"

"And a sip for you," he said, lifting her head from the bed and holding her as he tipped the mouth of the bottle to her lips. She took a long drink, easing the dryness in her mouth before she raised up and kissed him. She tasted him, the wine and passion.

And she wanted more.

"Are you ready?" he asked, easing her down and setting the bottle back on the table.

"Oh, I think so," she said, reaching for him.

He shook his head, caught her hands in his and said, "Then find something to hold onto."

He lowered his head to her breasts again and Rachel took his advice. Reaching back, she grabbed hold of the headboard and clung to it like a life rope tossed into a stormy sea. He sucked at her nipples, then moved down, licking the champagne off her skin as he went. Across her ribs, down over her abdomen and into the tiny pool of wine in her belly button.

She sucked in air, groaned out his name and held on even tighter. Her skin was on fire. Heat coiled inside and threatened to burst free. She felt every single nerve ending alive and hopping and oh, she hoped it never stopped.

He shifted position, moving to kneel between her legs, and Rachel smiled, eager for him to enter her again. Eager to feel the race to completion crowding in on her one more time.

But he had another surprise for her. Scooping his

hands beneath her bottom, he lifted her hips off the bed and smiled at her.

Her stomach did a quick somersault.

"Shane—"

"Hang on tight, Rachel," he whispered deeply. "This ride's about to get bumpy."

Five

His mouth covered her and Rachel groaned, his name sliding from her throat on a whisper of wonder. She watched him take her, couldn't look away. She concentrated on the feel of his hands on her behind, the lush sensation of his mouth, the hush of his breath.

Outside, the wind tossed snow against the frosted windowpanes. But inside, she was half surprised not to see steam rising from the bed.

Again and again, his lips and tongue worked her flesh, firing her blood, fuzzing her brain. She couldn't think. Couldn't remember *ever* thinking.

She was simply a mass of sensation. Her nerves stretched to the breaking point and hovered there as the tension in her body built and screamed through her, demanding release. Demanding satisfaction. Demanding his body inside hers.

Now.

"Shane," she managed to croak despite the tightness in her throat. "I want— I need you in me. Please."

He set her down and moved to cover her. "I need that, too," he whispered and wrapping his arms around her waist, he held onto her as he rolled onto his back.

And Rachel was straddling him, looking down into his eyes, feeling herself drowning in a sea of gold-flecked green.

She moved on him and Shane bit back a groan. In the lamplight pooling in through the windows, she looked like a goddess. Her honey-blond hair loose and waving about her shoulders, her breasts high and full, a knowing smile on her luscious mouth.

Something beyond lust, beyond desire quickened inside him. But it was forgotten in a new rush of need as she moved on him again. Swiveling her hips, she took him deep inside her body and sighed with satisfaction as she set a slow, steady rhythm between them.

He reached up, cupping her breasts and tweaking her nipples with his thumbs and forefingers. She sighed and that soft sound filled him with fire. He dropped his hands to her hips and guided her on him, helping her move.

Pushing himself higher and deeper inside her, he felt the first shuddering ripples of her climax wash through her. He saw her eyes glaze over, watched as her head fell back, and when she called his name,

Shane's body erupted and he jumped into oblivion, holding her close as he fell.

Rachel woke up a couple of hours later. She opened her eyes and found herself staring at the floor. Clinging to the edge of the mattress, she was cold and realized that not only had Shane hogged the bed, he'd also stolen all the blankets.

A sign?

Sliding off the bed, she hurried to the closet, threw it open and grabbed her robe. With the thick, dark green terry cloth wrapped around her, she tied the belt at her waist and looked at Shane, sprawled across her mattress. Torn between the glow of having been well loved and already worrying about how in the hell she would ever be able to look him in the eye again, Rachel chewed at her bottom lip. Her mind raced with possibilities and consequences.

None of them pleasant.

She wasn't an idiot.

She knew darn well that the hours they'd spent together in her bed wouldn't mean to Shane what it had to her.

Sure, they'd made something magical between the two of them, but he wasn't in love with her. She knew that.

What she didn't know was why he'd—

Stop.

Rachel shut her brain off, refusing to continue wandering down the twisted paths her mind kept showing her. It was too late to turn back the clock and prevent this night from happening, even if she wanted to. Which, to be honest, she didn't.

Turning her back on Shane, she slipped from the bedroom and walked quietly through the darkness. She paused in the living room long enough to turn off the stereo, then continued on to the kitchen, moving through a silence so loud it was deafening.

There, she moved around the familiar space, not needing a light. She filled the coffeepot with water, set it back on the hot plate and filled the basket with a few scoops of dark, rich Colombian coffee grounds. She hit the button and stood in the shadows as the coffeemaker hissed and gurgled, scenting the air with an aroma that was both comforting and familiar.

She stared out the window and nearly hypnotized herself watching snow drifting past the glass. Her body still hummed with satisfaction and yet…she couldn't settle. Couldn't enjoy even the memories of what she and Shane had shared. Because she knew that with the morning light, everything between them would be changed.

Forever.

What she *didn't* know was what to do about it.

Rubbing her hands up and down her arms against a chill she felt right down to her bones, she walked back to the bedroom, opened the door quietly and stood on the threshold. He was still sleeping, so Rachel indulged herself and watched him unnoticed as he slept.

Something inside her turned over and she realized that sleeping with him had only intensified her feelings. And she wondered what in the heck she was supposed to do now.

How could she look at him again, knowing what it was like to be in his arms, and pretend she didn't want it to happen again?

How could she face him at work and *not* remember his kiss, his body wrapped around hers?

"You're watching me."

His voice rumbled from the shadows and she jumped. "Didn't know you were awake."

He rose up and braced himself on his elbows. The quilt covering him slid down his broad, naked chest and puddled at his hips. She couldn't see his eyes in the dark, but she felt his gaze as surely as if he'd reached out to touch her.

Oh, she was in such deep trouble.

"I smelled the coffee."

Of course he did. He hadn't been reacting to some secret sense telling him she was nearby. They weren't *connected* on some higher emotional plane, for Pete's sake.

She swallowed regret and grimaced at the bitter taste. "It's ready if you want some."

"Sounds good."

Well, isn't this nice and stiff, she thought. Any more polite and there'd be icicles hanging in the air between them. But she didn't say that. What would be the point? She only nodded and left, knowing he'd get up and follow her.

It took him a few minutes and when he walked into the now brightly lit kitchen, he was dressed, his suit coat slung across one shoulder hooked on his index finger. He laid the jacket down over the back of a chair, then took the coffee mug she offered him.

"Thanks."

"You're welcome." How very dignified they were, when only a couple of hours ago, they'd been all over each other.

"It's good," he said after taking a sip.

Rachel tugged at the collar of her robe, feeling at a real disadvantage with him in his suit and her...well, naked under a layer of terry cloth. To occupy herself, she reached for her own coffee cup and folded both hands around it. Taking a long sip, she let the heat shoot through her before she spoke again.

Then, keeping her voice light despite the ball of lead settled in the pit of her stomach, she said, "So when does everyone else get to hear the news about your big win at EPH?"

He studied the surface of his coffee. "My father's going to officially announce it at the New Year's party."

"But word will get out to the family long before then."

"Probably," he agreed, a half smile on his face.

"You're looking forward to your brothers and sister finding out."

"Of course. And you should, too."

She leaned back against the edge of the counter. "Why's that?"

"Because we're a team, Rachel," he blurted, then let his voice trail off and his gaze drift back to his coffee.

Awkwardness rose up and sat between them like an ugly troll waiting to be recognized.

So Rachel did.

"We're not a team, Shane. I work for you."

His gaze snapped to hers. "Yeah, but—"

She set her coffee down on the countertop and stuffed both hands into the pockets of her robe. Her bare toes curled on the cold floor. "What happened between us tonight—"

"Was a mistake, I know," he said and Rachel's jaw dropped.

"Well, that was honest."

He set his coffee down on the small table, pushed his hands into his slacks pockets and started pacing. A few steps to the counter, then a few steps back again.

"It was my fault," he said, his voice gruff, laced with an emotion she couldn't identify. "And it shouldn't have happened. Damn it, Rachel, you *work* for me—"

"That's right," she said firmly, fighting back the quaver wanting to sound in her voice. "I *work* for you—but I make my own decisions. And last night was as much about *my* choices as yours."

He blew out a breath. "Fine. We both decided. But I should have been the one to back off."

A choked laugh shot from her throat. "Oh, yes. The big strong man should have found a way to save the little woman from herself. Is that it?"

His features tightened up and the muscle in his jaw twitched. "Damn it, that's not what I meant."

"I'm not so sure." Heck, she wasn't sure of anything at the moment. All she knew for a fact was she wanted him out of her house before she did something really stupid like cry.

Oh, wouldn't that be the cherry on top? Sleep with your boss then cry about it in front of him. Hey, atta girl Rachel, she told herself. Keep doing dumb stuff.

God, this conversation was even harder than she'd thought it would be when she was simply dreading it.

He glanced at his wristwatch, then to her. "Maybe we shouldn't try to talk about this now."

She nodded stiffly. "Maybe not."

"I should probably go."

"Good idea." Go already, she screamed inwardly. Hurry it up before the tears start.

God, she felt like an idiot.

But she'd brought this on herself. She was the one who kissed *him*. Heck, after that, of course he had to have sex with her. Turning her down would have been embarrassing. How much kinder to just sleep with the poor little lonely assistant.

A pity romp.

Great.

What every girl dreams of.

He picked up his jacket and shrugged into it. Straightening the collar and lapels, he looked at her and oh God, she saw concern in his eyes.

Concern. So close to sympathy.

To pity.

"I'll see you at work later?"

She lifted her chin, and forced herself to speak

past the knot in her throat. "Sure. I may be a little late because—"

"Doesn't matter," he interrupted. "Take your time. In fact, take the morning off. Come in this afternoon."

He was in no hurry to face her at work, was he? "Fine. I'll see you later."

He nodded and looked for a second as if he wanted to say something more. Thankfully he thought better of it and walked away. When he left the apartment, he closed the door quietly behind him. And Rachel was alone.

Again.

Shane tried to keep his mind on the job, but it wasn't easy. For one thing, every time he passed Rachel's empty desk, he remembered why she wasn't there.

Of course, if she *had* been there, it would have been even harder to walk past her desk. What an idiot he was. What had he been thinking?

He hadn't been thinking at all. Just reacting. To some really incredible feelings. To the press of Rachel's mouth to his. To the rush of holding her in his arms. He muttered an oath, pushed one hand through his hair and told himself to stop remembering. To stop reliving those hours with her.

He might as well take a vow to not breathe.

Restless, Shane pushed away from his desk and turned to stare out the windows. Snow was still falling, with more predicted. On the street far below him, people were rushing down sidewalks, oblivious to the cold. Twinkling lights lined the storefronts and he imagined the street corner Santas were doing a booming business.

It was the end of a long year. His family was closer than they'd ever been and he'd earned the CEO position at the company. By rights, he should be celebrating right now. Instead he felt as though he'd lost something important.

"Crisis! Crisis!"

Shane spun around to face Jonathon Taylor as he gave a perfunctory knock and hustled into the office. "What's wrong?"

"Oh, only the end of my Fourth of July spectacular, that's all." Jonathon lifted both hands dramatically into the air before letting them fall to his sides again.

Good. Business. A chance to concentrate on something besides Rachel. Folding his arms across his chest, Shane watched as the other man paced frenetically around the office. "What happened?"

"My queen," Jonathon moaned theatrically, "my star of the issue—Leticia Baldwin—"

"Ah…" Shane walked back to his desk and sat down. Letty Baldwin, the latest of America's sweethearts. A young actress with talent as well as beauty. "She won't do the article?"

"Oh, she'll do it," Jonathon pouted as he dropped into the chair opposite Shane's desk. "But she's going to be seven months pregnant when it's time to do the photo shoot. Can't exactly use the red, white and blue bikini theme I had in mind. This is just a disaster, Shane. She was my centerpiece. My star. My—"

"—queen, yeah I get it."

He slumped lower in his chair, his spine becoming an overcooked noodle. "I'm shattered."

Shane laughed.

Jonathon glowered at him. "I'm so happy to amuse you."

"Sorry," Shane said, lifting both hands to appease his friend. "It's just that I really needed this little crisis of yours, that's all."

"At least one of us is happy."

"Jon," Shane said, leaning back in his chair, "does Letty Baldwin still want to do the issue?"

"Oh, definitely. Her agent's convinced her that it would be good exposure. And it would, of course."

"Then do it now."

"What?"

"The photo shoot," Shane said slowly, patiently. "Set it up with Ferria and Letty's people. Do the shoot now and just sit on the pictures until the issue's ready to go to press."

Jonathon's features smoothed out as he thought about it. "We could, couldn't we?"

"As long as she agrees, I don't see why not."

"Sandy will throw a fit," Jonathon mused, and seemed to enjoy the idea. "She's already shrieking over the expenses for this quarter."

"I'll handle Sandy," Shane assured him, making a mental note to call his managing editor and smooth over any ruffled feathers.

"Brilliant," Jonathon shouted and bounded from his chair, rubbing his palms together. "This, my king, is why you're in charge."

As Jonathon left, Shane could only wish that all of his problems were so easily solved.

Six

Rachel carried a cup of coffee into Shane's office and braced herself before meeting his gaze. She needn't have worried. After stalling around for three hours, she'd finally come into work, only to be so busy she hadn't had to face Shane all afternoon.

Until now.

Every day at four-thirty, he had a cup of coffee while going over the day's reports, bringing himself up to speed on the different divisions and setting up appointments for the following day. It was a routine. One she'd long since become familiar with.

In fact, over the last few years, she'd come to enjoy this last half hour of the workday. It gave her a chance to relax with a man she both loved *and* liked. Of course, today there'd be no relaxing.

She felt as though every nerve in her body was strung tight and plugged into an electrical outlet.

He looked up as she entered and gave her a distracted smile. "Come on in, Rachel."

She carried the cup of coffee to him and set it down on his desk. Tension arced between them with all the dazzling light and power of a lightning strike. She could almost hear the sizzle in the air.

"How are you?"

"I'm fine, Shane," she said, lying through her teeth. But damned if she'd slink around the office. "And you?"

He reached for the coffee cup, but instead of picking it up, he trailed the tips of his long fingers over the curved handle. Rachel's gaze locked on the movement, and in an instant, her body lit up as she remembered the feel of those fingers on her skin.

Okay, this was going to be a touch more difficult than she'd thought.

"Worried," he said finally and she shifted her gaze to his.

"About...?"

He scowled at her. "About *us,* Rachel. About our working relationship."

She felt a warm flush of embarrassment move through her and she could only hope it wasn't blazing on her face. This was so not fair. She'd dreamed about Shane for over a year, had imagined what a night with him would be like. And now those dreams had become nightmares.

All she had left was her pride and she was going to cling to it with everything she had. "Our working relationship doesn't have to change at all, Shane," she said and hoped to heaven she sounded more sure than she felt.

"Is that right?" He stood up, pushed the edges of his suit jacket back and shoved both hands into his slacks pockets. "So, everything is normal."

"That's right."

"Then why haven't you ragged on me once about work?"

"Excuse me?"

"Normally you'd have come in here carrying that memo pad that's practically stapled to your hand," he pointed out. "And you'd be reading me the list of meetings to go to, warning me about which ones I couldn't duck. Any other day, you'd be standing there telling me who to call, when to do it and what to say."

Rachel sniffed, a little irritated that he knew her so well. But then, they were a team, weren't they? A well-oiled machine. It wasn't *his* fault that she'd fallen in love with him and changed everything. "I'm so very sorry. I had no idea I was that bossy."

He pulled one hand free of his pockets and waved at her. "Bull. Of course you did." He came around the edge of his desk and started toward her. But he stopped a few steps short, as if he couldn't quite trust himself to get too close.

Oh, you're dreaming girl, she told herself. It

was probably more like he was afraid his too aggressive assistant would jump his bones again if he wandered too near.

God help her, he was probably right.

"But that's why we've always worked together so well," he was saying and Rachel shut down her brain and opened her ears. "You keep me focused on the job and I give you somebody to nag."

"Very nice," she muttered.

"And now it's ruined," he snapped.

"Maybe that's for the best."

"Like hell it is," Shane said grimly. "How the hell can I get anything done when I can damn well *feel* the tension between us?"

Okay, she'd made up her mind earlier to be aloof. Distant. To do what she could to pretend that last night had never happened. But now that Shane had pried the lid off this particular can of worms, why should she try to jam the lid back on?

"You're not the only one, you know. Forgive me," she said, "for being just a little on edge. It's not every day I have to face my boss after he's seen me naked."

Shane winced. "I could say the same."

"Yeah," she agreed, "but from my perspective, this is just a little bit harder."

"How's that?"

She laughed shortly and felt the sound scrape against her throat. "This is a cliché for God's sake. Employers have been diddling with their secretaries/assistants for generations!"

"Diddling?"

"Don't you dare smile at me," she shot back. "Diddling is a perfectly good word."

"You're right," he said and took one cautious step closer. "But don't you lump me in with some sleazy guy who makes a habit of sleeping with his secretary."

"Assistant."

"Fine. Assistant." He shoved one hand through his hair and Rachel remembered how soft his thick, dark brown hair was. How it felt streaming through her fingers. She swallowed hard.

"My point," he continued, his voice hardly more than a growl, "is that what happened between us shouldn't have happened at all."

"Yes," she said tightly, "I believe you covered that this morning with the whole 'mistake' thing."

"Well, wasn't it?"

Her hands at her sides, she curled her fingers into her palms and squeezed until she felt the indentation of every nail digging into her skin. *Mistake?* No doubt. Did she regret it? She certainly should. But she couldn't honestly say she did.

She'd wanted him for so long how could she possibly regret having him? Even if it meant having to deal with the messy repercussions.

Watching his face, trying to read the maelstrom of emotion in his eyes, Rachel said, "Of course it was."

Was that disappointment flashing across his eyes? If it was, it was gone almost immediately.

He nodded, blew out a breath and said quietly, "At least we agree on that."

"Yay us."

A half smile quirked the corner of his mouth then disappeared again. "The question is, can we work past it? Can we just forget about what happened and go back to the way things were?"

"I don't know," she said honestly after a long, thoughtful pause. "I'd like to think so."

A small thread of panic jolted through Shane as he watched her. He'd called their time together a mistake. But he didn't regret it. How could he? He'd never experienced anything like what he'd found with Rachel.

He'd been thinking of nothing *but* her for hours. And now that she was standing there in front of him it took every ounce of self-control he possessed to keep from grabbing her and kissing her until neither of them was able to think.

But that wouldn't solve a damn thing. It would in fact, only make a weird situation even more uncomfortable.

"Rachel, I don't want to lose what we have. Our friendship."

"I think that ship has sailed, Shane." Her mouth curved sadly.

"I don't accept that."

Her green eyes filled with tears and he held his breath, hoping to hell they wouldn't fall. He was a dead man if she started crying. Nothing in this world could bring a man to his knees faster than a strong woman's tears.

As if she heard his panicked thoughts, she blinked quickly, furiously, and kept her tears at bay.

"You have to, Shane," she said, with a slow shake of her head. "If we hope to salvage this working relationship, we both have to accept the facts. We're not friends. We're not lovers. To be honest, I'm not sure what we are anymore."

After work, Shane was too irritable to go home alone and not in a good enough mood to call a friend. That last conversation with Rachel kept rewinding and playing in his mind and he couldn't quite seem to settle with it. Things were different between them now and he didn't have a clue what to do about it.

It had been a long time since he'd let his groin do his thinking for him.

Now he remembered *why*.

If he hadn't given in to his own desires the night before, everything in his world would be running great. He'd won the competition in the family, *The Buzz* was gaining strength every damn day and he'd finally realized that he was doing *exactly* what he should be doing.

He stepped out of the EPH building into a face full of wind-driven snow. Shrugging deeper into his overcoat, he squinted into the wind and glanced around. The sidewalks were crowded, as usual. Manhattan streets were never quiet. Cabs carried customers, buses belched along the street and a police squad car, lights flashing, siren whining, fought to get through the congestion.

He loved it.

Loved the noise, the hustle, the rush of life that pulsed in the city like a heartbeat. Stepping out onto the sidewalk, he fell into step with the crush of people instantly surrounding him. You had to keep up when walking these sidewalks. Move too slowly and the crowd would knock you down and kick your body to the curb, all without losing step.

Smiling to himself, he realized he was in the perfect frame of mind for walking in Manhattan.

He wasn't sure where he was going, he just knew he didn't want to go home. God knew there were plenty of women he could call for company, but that thought left him a lot colder than the melting snow sliding beneath his coat collar.

Hands in his pockets, he let his gaze drift while his mind raced. Strings of twinkling lights lined the front windows of the shops he passed, and the combined scents of hot chocolate, steaming coffee and hot dogs poured from a street vendor's cart. He came to the end of the block and while he stood waiting for the light to change, he glanced in the front window of Hannigan's.

A bar that was too upscale to be called a tavern, but too down to earth to be classified a club, Hannigan's offered cold beers and friendly conversation. Sounded a hell of a lot better than going home alone.

Shane marched to the door, pulled it open and was slapped with a blast of warmth, coated with laughter and the jangling beat of Irish folk music.

He shrugged out of his coat, hung it on the rack by the door, then made his way through the tangled maze of tables and chairs.

The hardwood floors were gleaming, a fire danced in the stone hearth on the far wall and behind the polished mahogany bar, a gigantic mirror reflected the faces of the patrons.

Shane pushed through the crowd, made his way to the bar and leaned both elbows on the shining top. When the bartender worked his way down to him, he said quickly, "Guinness."

In a few minutes, the practiced barman was sliding over a perfectly built drink, with a thick layer of cream colored foam atop dark, rich beer. Shane picked up the glass, took a sip and turned to look at the crowded room. His gaze slid across a few familiar faces; after all, everyone who worked in the neighborhood ended up in here at one time or another.

At a booth in the back sat a man more familiar than the rest. Shane headed that way, deftly avoiding a waitress with a laden tray. He tapped on the tabletop, waited for his nephew to look up at him in welcome, then slid into the booth opposite him.

Gannon Elliott was a big man, with black hair, sharp green eyes, and in the last year or so, a ready smile. At thirty-three, Gannon was only five years younger than Shane. The two had grown up more like brothers, though Gannon was his nephew, the son of Michael, Shane's oldest brother.

"Didn't expect to see you in here, Gannon."

The other man shrugged. "Erika wanted to do some Christmas shopping," he said, sliding his half full glass of beer back and forth on the tabletop. "Hannigan's sounded like a better idea to me."

"Christmas shopping." Shane slumped back against the red leather booth. "Haven't started that yet."

"My suggestion?" Gannon quipped, lifting his glass for a long drink. "Get married. Turns out women *like* shopping."

Shane smiled, both at the ridiculous notion of getting married and at the change in his nephew. Only a year ago, Gannon would still have been at work, staying late into the night. More like his grandfather Patrick than any of Patrick's kids were, Gannon had lived and breathed the family business.

Until Erika.

"What about you? Why are you sitting here having a drink with me?" Gannon took another swallow of his beer. "Why aren't you out with that Hollywood girl...what's her name, Amber or Brownie or something?"

Shane frowned, thinking about the woman he was supposed to have had dinner with the night before. He *still* couldn't think of her damn name. But if he'd only met her as planned, none of that mess with Rachel would have happened and he wouldn't now be sitting in the middle of a mess.

"What is that woman's name?" he muttered. "Never mind. Anyway, I wasn't in the mood."

Gannon laughed. "*You?* Not in the mood for a gorgeous woman? You feeling all right?"

"Funny." He took a sip of Guinness and savored the taste.

"Didn't mean it to be funny," Gannon said, studying him now through shrewd green eyes. "Something going on? You should be happy as hell. Heard you won the CEO position."

Shane's gaze snapped to him. "Who told?"

Someone at the bar laughed loudly and the music changed, drifting from a ballad in Gaelic to a jittering rhythm that even had Shane's toes tapping in time.

"Hell," Gannon laughed, "who *doesn't* know? Everyone in the company pretty much had it figured out a few months back. When those third-quarter profit statements came in, it was clear no one was going to be able to catch you."

Pride rippled through Shane, but it didn't do a damn thing to ease the knot of something else tightening in his chest. "Thanks. It was a team effort, though. We *all* made it happen. Everyone at *The Buzz* worked their asses off."

"Which begs the question again," his nephew said. "You should be happier than hell right now. Why aren't you?"

"Long story."

"Do I look busy?"

Shane chuckled. "No, you don't." He nodded, paused for another sip of beer, then said, "Okay, but before we get into the sad, sad story of my life… How's your mom doing?"

Gannon's mother, Shane's sister-in-law Karen,

had been battling breast cancer for the last year. And after a double mastectomy and a debilitating round of chemotherapy, the family was hopeful that she'd beaten the cancer.

Gannon blew out a breath and smiled. "She's doing good. Great, in fact." He signaled the waitress by holding up his empty beer glass, then shifted his gaze back to Shane. "Dad's at her side round the clock. It's pretty amazing to see, really. They've…rediscovered each other, I guess you'd say. And even with the cancer threat hanging over us all, they're so damn happy, it's ridiculous."

"I'm glad."

"Yeah," Gannon said wistfully, "me, too." When the waitress brought him a refill and took away his empty glass, Gannon turned his gaze on Shane. "So, now that we've covered Mom, what's going on with you?"

Shane really didn't want to get into it with his nephew. But who the hell else would understand? Gannon and his wife, Erika, had started out working together—and had an affair. It had all blown up in their faces of course, but they'd finally found their way back to each other and now seemed happy as clams.

Whatever the hell *that* meant.

"Before I get into that," he said, easing into an uncomfortable conversation, "when you and Erika first started your…"

"Affair?"

"Okay." Shane nodded. "Was it hard to work together? Was it…clumsy? Awkward?"

Gannon scraped one hand across his face. "It

wasn't simple," he finally said. "But we both knew what we were doing. We both *chose* to have the affair. Even though it ended badly."

"So you didn't have trouble working together once you'd had sex?"

"If you mean could I keep from imagining her naked, then no. But we managed. For a while." He frowned to himself.

Shane knew what he was thinking about. Gannon was one of the most private men Shane had ever known. The idea of people gossiping about him was anathema to him. The minute talk had started up in the company about his affair with Erika, he'd called it off. Erika had quit soon after and it hadn't been easy for Gannon to talk her into coming back once the Elliott family competition had started last January.

It hadn't been easy, but Gannon had finally realized just what Erika meant to him. And now they were married, and already a week overdue to become parents for the first time. "How's Erika holding up?"

"*She's* doing great," Gannon admitted. "I'm the one who jumps every time she makes a sound. But the doctor said if she hasn't delivered by next Monday, he'll induce. Thank God."

"That's good. Good." Shane nodded, then said under his breath, "I think I've done something really stupid."

"Rachel?"

"Is that a good guess or is there already talk?"

"No talk." Gannon took a drink. "It's just that Fin used to tell me all the time about how perfect Rachel was for you only you were too dumb to see it."

"Ah," Shane mused, "good to be loved by your family."

"Hey, we love you even when you're stupid."

"Small consolation."

"So," Gannon continued, "I'm guessing that things are not really rolling right along now that the situation with Rachel's…changed."

"You could say that." He shook his head and stared up at the pierced tin ceiling. "Hell, Gannon, I don't even know what to say to her anymore. I keep thinking about last night and—" He shut up fast, but it was pointless, since his nephew already understood exactly what Shane was feeling. Been there, done that.

"Don't use me for a template, Shane," Gannon said tightly. "I almost lost Erika, so I'm sure as hell not the one to give you advice."

Shane took a long, deep drink of his beer, then set the glass down again carefully. "Yeah, but you *loved* Erika. Even when you were being an idiot, you loved her."

"You don't love Rachel?"

Love?

He'd never really thought about love. Always been too busy just having a good time. But in his bones, he knew damn well that Rachel was different. She wasn't just another woman in a long string of unremarkable relationships.

But love?

Shane sighed and signaled the waitress. "Damned if I know."

Seven

Ben & Jerry's was a sad substitute for sex with Shane. But, since it was all Rachel had, she indulged. Curled up on the couch, with the TV muted and showing some old black-and-white movie, she dug her spoon into the chocolate chunk ice cream. One bite after another slid down her throat despite the huge knot lodged there.

"Idiot," she muttered, pausing to lick her spoon. If she had any spine at all, she'd be out tonight, doing some Christmas shopping. Getting on with her life. Forgetting about Shane.

Apparently, though, her spine was pretty much a wet noodle.

She glanced around the room, sighing. But for the

three Hollyberry scented candles burning in a twisted metal candelabrum on top of the entertainment center, there were absolutely no decorations up. This just wasn't like her.

Ordinarily Rachel was a real Christmas nut. Nothing she liked better than dragging out all of the boxes filled with her Christmas goodies. Stuffed animals, three crèches, hand knit stockings she'd made during her knitting phase, silk garland and the wreath she'd made the Christmas before.

But no. She couldn't get her mind off her troubles long enough to care about the most magical season of the year.

"Just pitiful," she murmured and dipped her spoon back into the carton for another chunk of chocolate.

When the phone rang, she ignored caller ID and all but lunged for it, desperate to hear a voice other than her own. That feeling lasted less than ten seconds.

"Honey," her mother cooed in a voice pitched to carry over fifty thousand screaming fans in Yankee Stadium. "I'm so glad you're home!"

"Hi, Mom." Rachel swallowed fast and instantly took another bite of chocolate. She loved her mother, she really did. But every year about this time, Celeste Adler started in on the "you're not getting any younger" speech. Her mother was bound and determined to get her older daughter married and "settled." Rachel's younger sister, Rita, had been married two years and the "perfect" daughter was already pregnant. With twins.

So basically, even if Rachel got pregnant right this minute, Rita would still outdo her.

Pregnant.

For just an instant, she allowed herself a brief, tantalizing dream. One night with Shane and a baby to remember it by. Wouldn't that have been something? She sighed and took another bite of ice cream. No way. Her birth control pills were way too effective. Other women might have an accident, but Rachel wouldn't. Even her body was a rule follower.

"Rita had an ultrasound this morning and she let me come in with her and ohmygoodness—" that last was crammed into one breathless word "—it was the most exciting thing ever. You know, Rita's husband Jack is just the most wonderful man."

Rachel rolled her eyes. Jack would never be simply *Jack.* His full name from now unto eternity would be *Rita's Husband Jack.* Poor man. But then, she told herself as she crunched quietly on an extra big chunk of chocolate, no one had held a gun to his head. He'd dated Rita for two years. He knew exactly the kind of whacko family he was marrying into.

Not whacko in a bad way of course. She loved them all. But did she really need to hear a speech every year about how she was all alone? Thanks, no.

"He gave me a big hug and called me Grandma right there in the doctor's office, isn't that the sweetest thing?"

Suck-up, she thought, but said only, "Yep. Jack's a keeper."

"Oh my yes, and I just cried and cried. I'm so emotional about my girls, you know."

Rachel's spoon scraped the bottom of the carton and she frowned. Darn it. Only a couple bites left. She should have been more prepared. She knew darn well that her mother called every Wednesday night without fail. She should have stocked extra ice cream.

"I know, Mom."

"And Rita's thinking of naming one of the babies after me, if one is a girl, that is."

Great. Just what the world needed. Another Celeste.

"That's nice." Rachel tucked the phone between her neck and her shoulder and shifted a look at the television screen. *It's a Wonderful Life* was playing. Of course it was. It had become almost more of a tradition than Midnight Mass.

While her mother talked, Rachel concentrated on George Bailey's trials and tribulations. As he stood at the top of the bridge looking into the icy river, Rachel completely understood why he was considering the leap.

"So, honey, anything new to tell me?"

Rachel froze, silently thanking God that her mother was safely tucked up in her house in Connecticut. If Celeste was looking right at her, she could use her motherly psychic powers and know exactly what her daughter had been up to.

That was one humiliation she didn't have to suffer through, anyway.

"Nope," she said after way too long a pause, "same ol', same ol'…"

"Uh-huh, that's nice, dear. Did I tell you that Margie Fontenot's grandson Will is coming to town for Christmas this year?"

Oh God. She knew what was coming. Another fix-up. Frantically Rachel scraped at the ice cream carton, hoping for more chocolate—which she now so desperately needed. "Really?"

"Oh, yes," her mother continued excitedly, "he's a *doctor,* you know."

Oh man, Celeste's Holy Grail.

Hook a doctor for poor Rachel.

"That's nice," she said ambiguously, scrambling off the couch, clutching the empty ice-cream carton and spoon. Hustling into the kitchen, she tossed the carton into the trash, the spoon into the sink, then turned to the pantry. While her mother oohed and aahed over Margie's fabulous grandson, Rachel scrounged for cookies. Preferably *chocolate* cookies.

She settled for a stale Pop-Tart.

Taking a bite, she leaned against the counter and closed her eyes. Only have to hang on a few more minutes, she assured herself. Celeste's calls never went longer than ten minutes. Long distance charges, *donchaknow.*

"Anyway, honey," her mother said, then muttered, "oh Frank, go watch TV. Rachel knows I'm only trying to help." When she came back again, she said, "Your daddy says hello, honey."

Rachel smiled in spite of everything. God bless her father. Always trying to reel his wife in when her latest matchmaking attempt kicked in. "Hi back."

"She says hello. Yes," Celeste added, emphasizing the word with impatience, "I'll tell her to check her door locks."

Rachel grinned and chewed a rock-hard, cold toaster pastry. Her mom was only interested in romance or the promise of one. Her father, on the other hand, installed a new lock on Rachel's door every time they came to the city. Pretty soon she was going to have to buy an extra door to accommodate them all.

"Check your locks."

"Already done."

"Thank heaven." Celeste lowered her booming voice and Rachel knew it was because she was trying to avoid having her husband overhear. "Anyway, honey, we're giving a little party the weekend before Christmas this year. Nothing special. Just a few friends."

"Like Margie?" Rachel guessed, barely containing the helpless snarl as she tore off another chunk of dry Pop-Tart.

"Of course, honey, you know how fond I am of Margie," her mother went on, picking up speed as she finally reached her destination. "And of course, since Will is here in town visiting, he'll be attending, too. Won't that be nice? I just *know* you two will have so much in common."

Rachel sighed. "Where's he live?"

"Phoenix, I believe."

Well sure, Rachel thought. She lived in Manhattan and worked at a magazine. Will was a doctor living in Phoenix. So much in common it was uncanny. Almost eerie. Must be Kismet.

God, the pity just kept on coming. It was her own fault, though. If she hadn't spent so much time thinking about Shane, maybe she could have met someone else by now. Someone she actually might have a future with. She took another bite.

"Mom…"

"Now, don't you get your back up, young lady," her mother said, clearly hoping to disarm Rachel before she could get a head of steam going. "It's Christmas. It's a time for having friends and family together and we're *going* to be together. Understood?"

Rachel's chin hit her chest.

If she were George Bailey at this moment, she'd be jumping off that bridge. And if stupid Clarence saved her sorry butt, she'd just have to kill him.

But as much as she might like to refuse her mother's invitation, they both knew she wouldn't. She'd never missed Christmas with her family and she wasn't going to start now. "Understood, Mom. I'll be there."

"That's my girl," Celeste cooed again, gracious in victory. "So, would you like me to e-mail you a picture of the twins in utero?"

"Sure," she said. "Why not?"

After all, once those twins were born, they were going to take a lot of heat off of Rachel.

"I'll do that right away, honey. But first I have to call your sister and make sure she's all right."

"But you just saw her this morning." Rachel

frowned at the magnetized grocery list stuck to the refrigerator. Picking up a pen, she scrawled CHOCOLATE in capital letters and underlined it half a dozen times just for emphasis.

"Pregnant women need taking care of," her mother assured her.

"Okey dokey, then," Rachel said with a sigh. "Say hi to Rita for me."

"I will. Now good night, honey, and your dad just said for you to check your locks again. We love you!"

With those final words ringing in her ear, Rachel heard her mother hang up and then listened aimlessly to the dial tone humming frenetically. She loved her mother, but after one of these phone calls, Rachel always felt a little disappointed in her own life.

Or rather, her *lack* of a life.

Christmas time and the only romance in her future was a setup fixed by her *mother.*

Stabbing the power button, she turned the phone off and carried it and what was left of her stale treat into the living room. Once there, she curled up on the couch again and turned up the volume on the movie.

And if a few tears escaped and rolled silently down her cheeks, who but she would know about it?

Shane stood outside Rachel's apartment door and asked himself again what the hell he was doing there. He should have just gone home after leaving

Gannon in the bar. But instead, he'd found himself heading for Rachel's.

Which said exactly what?

That he was still uncomfortable with the way they'd left things at the office? That he still felt like a sleazy boss for having sex with his assistant? That he simply wanted to see her again?

Yes, to all of the above.

It wasn't a good idea, though, and he knew it.

And even as that thought shot through his brain, he lifted his hand and knocked on her door.

"Shane?" Her voice was muffled. "What're you doing here?"

He glanced up and down the hallway, then directly into the peephole he knew she was watching him through. "I wanted to talk to you, Rachel."

"About what?"

He didn't hear any locks turning and she sure wasn't opening the door.

"Do you think I could come inside?"

"Why?"

He blew out a breath, leaned into the peephole and said, "Because I don't want to have this conversation in the hallway."

"Fine."

At last, he heard the distinctive sounds of a chain being dragged off and several dead bolts clacking. When she opened the door, he stepped inside before she could change her mind.

"What do you want, Shane?"

He glanced quickly around the room, took a sniff

of Christmas-scented air, then turned his gaze on her. Her blond hair was loose, waving over her shoulders. She wore a white cut-off T-shirt and pale green sweatpants that hung low on her hips, baring several inches of flat, toned belly. She was barefoot and her toes were painted a dark, sexy red.

A blast of heat and need shot through him, rocking him to his bones.

She still had the door open, one hand gripping the knob as if for support. Her wary gaze was locked on him and Shane nearly regretted coming over here. Nearly.

"Afraid to close the door?" he teased. "Worried about what might happen?"

She slammed it shut. "No."

Turning her back on him, she walked to her sofa, sat down in one corner of it and drew her knees to her chest. Focusing her attention on the television set, she proceeded to ignore him. Completely.

What kind of twisted guy was he that he was enjoying this?

He took a seat on the sofa, too, but watched her instead of the TV. "I just thought we should talk."

"Ah," she said, not taking her eyes off the old movie on the television, "because it went so well earlier today."

"No, because it didn't."

She sighed, tightened her arms around her updrawn legs and said, "Shane, there's absolutely nothing left to say, you know?"

"We can't just leave it like this, Rachel."

Finally she shifted a look at him and he saw her eyes, green and soft, and felt a ripple of something warm move through him.

"I know," she said quietly. "I've been thinking about it all night."

Shane's insides fisted. He had a feeling he wasn't going to like what was coming next. The expression on her face warned him that whatever she was thinking, it wasn't pleasant. Still, he'd never been a coward. "And what did you come up with?"

"There's really only one thing to do."

"Yeah?" Wary now, he kept his gaze fixed on hers and saw regret flash quickly across the surface of her eyes. He braced himself and even then, he wasn't prepared for what she said next.

"I'm turning in my two weeks notice."

Eight

"**W**hat?"

It did Rachel's heart good to see how shocked he was by her resignation. But it didn't change anything. In the last couple of hours, she'd done a lot of thinking.

She'd sat through George Bailey's problems, watched the resolution and cried when Clarence got his wings. But somewhere during her movie marathon, she'd come to grips with what she knew she had to do.

Her heart ached, but there was simply no other reasonable option. If she stayed at *The Buzz*, working with Shane, she'd never be able to move on with her life. She'd always be in love with him. No other man would be able to compare to him, so she'd end up alone and watching old Christmas movies in the dark by herself.

So as painful as this was, there really wasn't any choice.

"What're you talking about?" Shane demanded, jumping to his feet and glaring down at her. "You can't quit."

"I just did." She met his gaze squarely and hoped he couldn't read on her face the misery she was feeling.

"This is your solution? Running away?"

"I'm not running, I'm sitting."

"If that's a joke, I'm not smiling."

"Neither am I," she said, unfolding her legs and pushing off the couch. Starting to feel just a little bit cornered, she made a move to walk into the kitchen, but Shane's hand on her upper arm stopped her in her tracks. She stared down at his hand for a long couple of seconds before lifting her gaze to his.

He let her go, jammed his hands into his pockets and muttered, "You can't quit on me, Rachel. Not because—"

"You can't even say it," she said with a slow shake of her head. "Because we had *sex,* Shane. And I think it's a pretty good reason to quit."

"I don't." He pulled his hands free of his pockets, scooped them both through his hair, then let them fall to his sides. "Damn it, we're a team. We work great together. You really want to throw away four good years because of one night?"

No. What she *wanted* was to have more than one

night, but she couldn't very well tell him that, now could she? Just as she couldn't tell him that it would be impossible for her to pretend indifference to him now that she knew what it was like to be in his arms. How could she arrange his dates with other women when her own heart would be breaking?

"No." One word, firmly spoken. "You don't need me, Shane. You won the competition. You're the head honcho now."

"Which means I'll need you even more."

"No, it doesn't. You're just *used* to having me there. You'll survive." She wasn't entirely sure she would, but that was her problem.

"Don't do this, Rachel."

"I have to."

"I won't accept your resignation."

She smiled. At the core of him, Shane Elliott would always have a healthy ego. "That won't stop me."

"What will?"

"Nothing."

He stepped in close. So close that the scent of his cologne reached for her, dragging her in closer for a deeper breath. She closed her eyes. If she looked up into those green eyes of his, she'd be lost. If she saw his mouth only inches from hers, she wouldn't be able to resist taking another taste of him.

His hands dropped onto her shoulders and she felt the heat of his touch slide deep within her.

"I won't stop trying to change your mind," he warned, his voice deep, ragged.

"I know that."

His hands tightened on her. "Look at me."

"I'd rather not," she admitted.

He sighed. "I came over here tonight to— I don't know. Apologize for last night?"

She winced.

He stroked one hand over her hair, his fingers sliding through the silky strands. "But now that I'm here with you again, an apology is the last thing on my mind."

"Shane—"

"Open your eyes, Rachel."

She did and instantly felt swamped by the emotions churning in his gaze. Her stomach dipped and rolled, her heartbeat jumped into a fast gallop and a curl of something warm and delicious settled low inside her. "Shane, this isn't a good idea."

"Probably not," he allowed, lowering his head infinitesimally.

She licked her lips, heard her blood humming in her veins and knew without a doubt that if she let him kiss her, she was only asking for more trouble. Being with him again would only make their inevitable parting that much harder.

And yet…

She'd wanted more than one night with him. This was her chance. This was her chance to have *him* seduce *her*. The night before had been her idea. Tonight, Shane was the one taking charge. Showing her how much he wanted her.

And if she couldn't have his love, then tonight, she'd settle for being wanted.

He kissed her and Rachel leaned into him, giving herself over to the glory of his mouth on hers. To the solid strength of him towering over her. To the feel of his hands sliding down her back and beneath the waistband of her pale green sweats.

His big hands cupped her bottom and pulled her tight against him. So tight that she felt his erection, hard and thick, pressed into her abdomen. Swirls of longing, of need swept through her like the ripples on a pond after a stone's been thrown in. Over and over again, sensations crested, fell and rose again.

She moaned and twisted her hips against his. In response, he pulled her even more tightly to him, grinding his mouth against hers. His tongue claimed her, mating with her own in a wild, frenetic dance of desire that pulsed in the air around them both.

Rachel's fingers dug into his shoulders and she held on for all she was worth. Her knees wobbled and the world tipped slightly off-center. But she didn't care. Nothing was more important than the feeling of Shane's arms around her, his body pressed to hers.

Laboring for air, Shane broke the kiss, stared down into her eyes and gave her butt a squeeze. "Yes?" he asked, his voice broken with need.

"Oh, yes," she said and leaped at him, wrapping her legs around his hips and hanging on as he started for her bedroom.

One corner of her brain couldn't believe she was

doing this again. Compounding one mistake with another exactly like it couldn't be the right thing to do. But then again, if she was quitting her job anyway, she might as well make the most of the time she had with the man she loved.

Reaching down between their bodies, she slid one hand down to the zipper of his slacks and when she pulled it down, he sucked in air like a dying man trying for one last gasp. Her fingers curled around the hard, thick length of him and he tucked his face into the curve of her neck. His teeth and tongue worked at her flesh as if the very taste of her meant life itself.

Rachel saw stars exploding behind her eyes. Every square inch of her body felt alive with sensation and almost too sensitized. And she wanted more.

Now.

"Can't wait," he muttered thickly and stopped just outside her bedroom door. He set her on her feet, dragged her clothes off and tossed them to one side, then lifted her again.

"No waiting," she agreed, wrapping her bare legs around his waist and hanging on.

He turned quickly, braced her back against the wall and when she rose up slightly in his arms, Shane pushed his body hard into hers. Rachel groaned as he filled her. Her body stretched to its limits to accommodate him, she bore down hard, taking him even deeper inside.

Bracing one hand on the wall to her side and one

hand on his shoulder, Rachel helped all she could, but Shane didn't need assistance. He took her weight and held her easily, lifting her up and down on his length until they were both tortured with a burning, fiery need that sizzled between them.

Again and again, he withdrew only to plunge into her depths one more time. His breathing was ragged, his eyes glazed. Rachel's heart pounded until it was nothing but a deafening roar in her own ears.

Shane couldn't think. Could hardly see. All he could do was feel. And what he was feeling was even more intense than anything he'd experienced the night before.

Most of the day, he'd tried to convince himself that the night with Rachel hadn't been as amazing as he remembered it. Now he knew that for the sad lie it was.

Rachel took him to places he'd never imagined. Made him feel things he'd thought himself incapable of. Made him want more.

Her body surrounded him, her mouth opened on a sigh and her eyes closed as the first wild, frantic pumping release jolted through her. He watched pleasure claim her for as long as he could and then finally, he allowed himself to follow after her.

She hung limp in his arms and Shane was grateful for the wall at her back. Otherwise, they'd both be lying in a puddle on the floor.

"You okay?" he whispered.

She chuckled. "I'll let you know when I get feeling back in my legs."

He smiled. "I hear that."

"Shane—"

He dropped his head to her shoulder. "Let's not start the 'mistake' talk again."

"Why not?" she asked quietly. "Seems appropriate."

He lifted his head and looked down into her eyes again. Strange, he'd never really noticed what a beautiful shade of green her eyes were before last night. And now he couldn't seem to tear his gaze away.

"I didn't come over here tonight to do this."

"I know that," she said and shifted position slightly.

That small movement was enough to wake his body up and stir fresh desire. He hissed in a breath and tightened his hold on her. "But I'm not sorry we did it."

She leaned her head back against the wall and inhaled sharply as he pushed his hardening body into her again, setting off a fireworks display of sensation. "No," she admitted, "I guess I'm not, either."

"Glad to hear that," he said tightly, pushing them away from the wall and starting for the bedroom again. "Because I don't think we're finished."

She shivered and lowered herself onto his length as hard as she could. "I think you're right."

He walked right up to the bed, reached down and dragged the quilt back, then fell onto the mattress, still fully clothed and deep within her body.

Rachel laughed and he noticed a tiny dimple in her right cheek. He'd never noticed that before, either.

"Maybe you should get undressed first," she said, then gasped when he rocked his hips against hers.

"After," he muttered and rolled to his back, taking her atop him where he could watch her. "I'm not stopping now."

"Good idea." Smiling, she reached for the hem of her little T-shirt and whipped it up and off, tossing it into the shadows of the small room. Then, watching him, she covered her breasts with his hands and twisted her hips on him, creating an unbelievable friction that stole his breath.

Riding him, she took him places he'd never thought to go and couldn't wait to visit again. The bed beneath him was soft and smelled of lavender. The woman above him was amazing and her scent was soap, shampoo and woman.

Like a man possessed he guided her hips, steering her into a mind-numbing rhythm. She was the only thing in the world he could see. Feel. And all too soon, an explosion burst up between them, leaving his body shattered, his bones shaken and his heart quivering.

Two hours later, they were naked, lying in a pool of white, thrown through the windows from the streetlights outside. Rachel stared at the ceiling and listened to Shane's ragged breathing.

Her own heartbeat was racing and her body was still sizzling when she acknowledged that once again, she'd been an idiot. But how could she possibly have turned him down, when all she'd been able to think about since the night before was being with him again?

Despite how wonderful her body felt, her heart

was aching. By giving in to the urge to be with him, she was only setting herself up for more pain.

This had to stop.

"You're thinking," he murmured.

"Aren't you?" she countered.

"No." He turned his head on the pillow to look at her. Reaching out, he skimmed one hand across her bare belly and Rachel shivered. "When I'm with you I don't want to think. Don't want you to, either."

She sighed now. "*Not* thinking is what got us here in the first place."

"Exactly."

Eyes closed, she savored his touch for a second or two, indulging herself. Oh, she wanted him to take her again. Wanted to take *him* again. And because she wanted it so badly, she rolled out from under his touch and slid off the bed.

Now that her blood wasn't on fire, she could think more clearly. And though it broke her heart to admit it even to herself, she knew that being wanted would never be enough for her.

She wanted love.

She wanted family.

And she would never get that from Shane.

He blew out a frustrated breath and pushed himself up onto one elbow. "Rachel—"

"Shane, this just can't keep happening," she said, turning to find her clothes, then snatch them up off the floor. In the pale wash of light, she pulled her T-shirt on, then struggled into her sweats, hopping first on one foot, then the other. When she was finished, she picked up Shane's clothes, too, and tossed them at him.

He grabbed at them then dropped the pile onto the bed beside him. "You know, maybe there's a reason we keep ending up here."

Impatient with both herself and him, she huffed out a breath and shook her hair back from her face. "Oh, there's a reason all right. Neither one of us can be trusted."

He gave her a weary laugh. "You may have a point."

A stab of something cold and lonely poked at her insides but Rachel fought to ignore it. She wouldn't let him see what his simple statement had done to her. Instead she said, "This is why I had to quit, Shane. Why I *still* have to."

Muttering darkly, he rolled off the bed and stood up to get dressed. As he stepped into his clothes, he argued with her. "What we've had with each other has nothing to do with work."

"Of course it does." She planted her hands on her hips, lifted her chin and continued. "You know how it was today. We could hardly talk to each other."

"Didn't seem to have any trouble tonight."

"That—" she waved her hand at the bed "—is *not* talking."

He tossed his suit coat onto the rumpled mattress. "Rachel, you're making too big a deal out of this."

"And maybe you're taking it too lightly."

Shane pushed one hand through his hair and yanked while he went at it. The pain shooting through his skull was a small, but welcome distraction from the woman making him nuts. "What do you want me to say?"

So much, she thought, but didn't say. Oh, she wanted it all. She wanted him making love with her and *being* in love with her. But since she couldn't have one, she wouldn't have the other.

In the moonlight, his green eyes flashed with annoyance and something else she couldn't quite identify. Maybe it was just as well.

If nothing else, she at least knew that her decision to quit her job and move on had been a good one. Now all she needed was the courage to go ahead with the plan. Somehow, somewhere, she found the strength to straighten her spine.

"I want you to say you accept my resignation," she whispered.

He grabbed his jacket and shrugged into it. Tugging at the lapels until it hung right, he just stared at her for a long moment. Rachel held her breath and counted the seconds as they ticked past as steadily as a heartbeat.

Finally, though, Shane nodded. "If it's what you want."

Want? No.

Need? Yes.

"It is. Thanks."

"Right." He nodded, looked uneasily around the room, then focused his gaze on her again. "I'd better go. I'll see you at the office tomorrow?"

"I'll be there."

* * *

Long after Shane was gone, Rachel sat at her computer. Her fingers flew over the keys, as her eyes blurred with tears she refused to shed.

One last Tess Tells All column.

One more time, she'd write down her feelings for her boss. One more time, she'd pour out her heart and mask it with humor. And one more time, she'd watch Shane read it, chuckle at Tess's cleverness and never see himself in the words.

Nine

A few days later, Rachel was wishing she'd just quit her job outright.

Working with Shane and maintaining a stoic, distant attitude was harder than it sounded. He was polite, courteous and completely unreachable. She should have been glad that he was apparently as determined as she to not let their own desires erupt again.

Instead she was only irritated.

Wasn't this hard on him at all?

Shaking her head, she scrolled down the list of RSVP responses to the annual Elliott Christmas Charity Ball. Making notations on who had and hadn't responded yet, Rachel lost herself in the work. It was the one thing she could depend on now. And if this year's ball was going to be the last one she arranged, then by heaven, it was going to be the very best one anyone had ever seen.

Every year, EPH sponsored a charity extravaganza, raising money for women's shelters and children's hospitals in the city. And for the last four years, Rachel had been integral to the planning and execution of the ball. She kept track of invitations, caterers, musicians, decorations. She arranged for Santa to appear at the party for the children who would be attending and she made sure that Santa had exactly the right present for every child.

This was one job she was really going to miss when she left the company.

"Hey," Christina said. "Earth to Rachel."

She blinked and looked up at her friend. Christina's silver-framed glasses were riding low on her nose and her bright blue eyes were fixed on Rachel.

"I'm sorry. What?"

"Honey," Christina said, lowering her voice and bending down to lean both hands on Rachel's desk, "you have something you want to tell me?"

"What do you mean?"

The older woman took a quick look around, assuring herself that no one was close enough to overhear. Still, she lowered her voice another notch. "A new Tess Tells All column just left Production for the boss's office."

"Really?" Rachel tried to look surprised. "I thought that last column was it for her."

"Apparently she had one more in her," Christina said, narrowing her eyes thoughtfully, "and it was a beauty."

Rachel lowered her gaze, picked up a stack of files and busily straightened them as if clean edges meant her life. "Why're you telling me?"

"Nice try," her friend countered. "But you forget. I've got years of experience dealing with kids trying to hide things from me."

"Christina…"

"You're Tess."

"Shh!" Rachel looked around now and when she was sure they were alone, she stood up, motioned to Christina and headed for the break room. Her friend was just a step or two behind her and when they entered the empty room, Christina shut the door and leaned back against it.

"It's true."

Rachel grumbled a little as she automatically straightened the counter before grabbing a coffee cup and pouring herself some. "Yes. It's true. Happy?"

"Delirious. I've had my suspicions for a while now, but this column just confirmed it." Locking the door, she walked toward her friend, got herself some coffee and while she dumped several heaping teaspoons of sugar into the brew, she said, "I can't believe you didn't tell me."

"I couldn't tell anyone."

"I'm not just anyone."

"True," Rachel said, taking a sip of coffee. "And I wanted to tell you about me being Tess but—"

"Oh," Christina said waving one hand at her, "who cares about the Tess thing? I want to know why you didn't tell me you slept with Shane."

"Oh God." Dragging a chair out, Rachel fell into it and set her cup on the table.

"Talk, sweetie. I want details."

"No details. Please. I'm trying to forget them myself."

"Damn. That bad?"

Rachel laughed at the disappointment on her friend's face. "Hardly. That *good.*"

"Ooh. So why the long face?"

"Because everything's changed now."

"That's good," Christina said, then frowned. "Isn't it?"

"I quit my job."

"No, you did not."

"I had to," Rachel said, cradling her coffee cup between her palms, savoring the heat radiating through her. "I can't work with him now. It's just too hard."

"That's bull and you know it." Christina sighed and leaned back in her chair. "Quitting solves nothing."

"It gets me away from him."

"Honey, you'll *never* be able to get away from him. You'll keep on loving him even if you wander off to Timbuktu."

"Well, there's a happy thought," Rachel muttered. "Anyway, my resignation is in and so are a few applications I've managed to drop off on my lunch hour the last couple of days. There are lots of magazines here in the city," she continued, wanting to steer their talk away from Shane. "So it's not like I'll never see you again or anything."

"Damn straight on that," Christina said, giving her a tight smile. "But here's a question for you. What do you think Shane's going to say when he sees this column?"

Rachel laughed miserably, picked up her coffee and took a sip. "He's read dozens of 'em so far and hasn't recognized himself. Why should this time be any different?"

Christina picked up her own coffee cup and smiled at Rachel over the rim. "Oh, didn't I mention that part? You screwed up in this one. You actually referred to Tess's mystery boss as *Shane.*"

Rachel's cup fell from suddenly nerveless fingers and hit the tabletop with enough force to send waves of hot coffee washing over both women.

Shane had been fielding phone calls all morning. From agents of minor celebrities hoping to make a splash in *The Buzz,* to heads of major corporations wanting to talk product placement. Normally he would have fobbed off most of those calls to the proper departments.

But for the last few days, he'd been doing everything he could to keep busy. Even if it meant getting back into the trenches. The plan was to keep himself so preoccupied he wouldn't have time to think about Rachel.

It wasn't working.

She was always there, right at the edges of his mind, waiting for a quiet moment to pop in and torture him. Damn it, he'd managed to work with Rachel—closely—for four long years. In all that time, he'd never looked at her as he would any other wildly attractive woman.

She'd just been there. Like an extension of himself. Part of his office, his work world. And in the last year, since his father had kicked off this ridiculous competition, she'd been the one to give him a kick in the can when he needed it. Hell, he was just as responsible as he for *The Buzz* winning the competition. Maybe more so. Because Rachel was always on top of things. She'd kept his life running smoothly for four years and he'd never even noticed her beyond being grateful for the help.

How the *hell* could he have been so blind?

How could he not have noticed her eyes, her mouth, her sense of humor, her legs, her agile mind, her breasts, her loyalty, her behind?

And why was he noticing all of that *now?*

Muttering darkly, he stalked across his office when the phone started ringing again. But this time, instead of answering, he let it ring and walked to the bank of windows behind his desk.

When the phone stopped ringing, he smiled grimly only to turn and frown at the quick knock on the door. Before he could call out for whoever it was to leave, the door swung open and Rachel was there.

Her blond hair was pulled back and twisted into

some sort of elegant braid she usually did. But now he'd seen it hanging loose and waving around her face and that was how he pictured her. In his mind's eye her plain, pale green business suit was replaced by a skimpy T-shirt and a pair of green sweats.

Oh man, he was in deep trouble here.

"You okay?" she asked, frowning at him.

"Fine." Or at least, he would be if he could shut off his brain. "What is it?"

Before she could answer, another woman sailed past Rachel into his office and demanded, "What makes you so crabby, I'd like to know?"

"Mom," he said and felt a smile warm his face.

Maeve Elliott was a tiny woman physically, but her personality made her seem larger than life. She'd married Shane's father when she was a nineteen-year-old seamstress in Ireland. And, though Shane could take exception to the way Patrick had ignored his children from time to time, the old man had always treated his wife as if she were the most price-less treasure on the planet. Which, Shane admitted silently, she was.

He came around the desk, enfolded her in a quick, tight hug, then stepped back to look at her. Impec-cable as always, she wore a Chanel suit of icy-blue and her nearly all-white hair was swept up into an intricate knot on top of her head.

"So," she said, eyeing her son, "my question stands. Why so crabby, Shane?"

He frowned and shifted a look at Rachel, still standing in the doorway. "Just…busy."

"Then I won't keep you long," his mother said, half turning to motion Rachel into the office. "I just wanted to stop and tell you the news!"

Rachel came closer and Shane swore he caught a whiff of her scent. Just enough to tantalize. To tweak his memory of their last night together. To remind him there wouldn't be any other nights like it.

He bit back a scowl and focused on his mother, practically vibrating with energy. "What is it?" he teased. "Win the Mrs. America pageant, did you?"

"Ah, you were always the smooth one," she said, laughing. "No, no. Much better news. Our Erika's had her baby. A beautiful little girl she is, too. I'm a grandmother!"

"That's terrific," Shane said, meaning every word.

"Wonderful," Rachel added, smiling. "How's the new mom doing?"

Maeve smiled even wider. "Erika's doing just fine. It's Gannon who's having the breakdown. Poor love. Apparently being a witness to his wife's labor has left him flattened."

"Did he faint?" Shane asked, hoping for some good ammunition to tease Gannon with in the future.

"Of course not," Maeve said with a sniff. "It's just very hard seeing someone you love in pain."

"Yeah," Shane said, slanting a look at Rachel only to find her gaze on him. "It must be."

A second or two of silence stretched out between them and hummed with energy until even Maeve was affected by it. As she looked from one of them to the other, one perfectly arched brow lifted slightly. Delicately she cleared her throat until she had her son's attention again.

"I'll let you get back to work now, Shane darlin'," she said. "I'm just on my way to see your father and force him to take me to lunch."

Shane tore his gaze from Rachel and scrambled for equilibrium. Blowing out a breath, he took his mother's arm and said, "Why don't I join you? You can tell me all about the new Elliott."

"That would be lovely," she said, lifting one hand to touch his cheek. Then she turned to Rachel. "Would you like to accompany us as well, Rachel?"

"No," she said quickly, with a shake of her head. "I'll, um, just stay here and get a few things finished."

"Shame," Maeve said thoughtfully, then walked from the office, her son and Rachel right behind her.

With Shane gone for at least an hour, Rachel did something she'd never done before in all the four years she'd worked at *The Buzz*.

She rifled Shane's desk.

"For pity's sake, where would he put the blasted thing?" She yanked open the first two drawers in his desk, quickly thumbed through the folders and looked under the books and magazines stored there.

Nothing.

The bottom file drawer yielded no happier results.

She zipped through the stacks of folders atop his desk, her fingers flipping through the pages as her gaze swept the printed pages. But the new Tess column was nowhere to be found. Which left only one possibility.

Her gaze drifted to the locked drawer on the bottom left of the big desk. There was no way for her to get inside it. And if she *did* lose her mind and try to pick the lock, Shane would notice and then the jig would be up, anyway.

"How could I have been so stupid?" she wondered aloud and just managed to keep from thumping herself in the forehead with the heel of her hand.

Shane would read the column, know exactly who wrote it and would probably fire her on the spot. Of course, since she'd already resigned, it wouldn't carry a lot of weight. But oh, God. The embarrassment quotient was just too high to think about!

Mentally she raced back over the other columns she'd turned in for publication. All the times she'd talked about her boss in less than stellar terms. All the times she'd complained about his too active social life.

Her toe stopped tapping against the floor and her mouth dropped open. And the last column, where she'd admitted to feeling too much about him.

"This is a *disaster.*"

Dropping her head into her hands, she wished for a hole to open up under her feet and swallow her.

By the time Shane returned from lunch, tension bubbled inside him like a thick, poisonous brew.

Luckily enough, Rachel was gone from her desk, probably taking a late lunch herself. Just as well. He was in no mood for yet another stiff, polite exchange of empty pleasantries.

Especially after spending the last two hours dodging Maeve Elliott's questions.

God knew he loved his mother, but there was nothing the woman liked better than digging into her children's lives. Whether they welcomed it or not.

He'd been able to dodge her thinly veiled questions about his and Rachel's relationship—but just barely. And if his father hadn't insisted on talking about the company, Maeve wouldn't have given up until she'd pried every last ounce of information from him.

He stepped into his office, closed the door behind him and gratefully went back to work. At his desk, he unlocked the bottom drawer, pulled out the latest columns sent to him by Production, and leaned back in his chair to flip through them.

When he found the Tess column, he smiled to himself, put the other articles aside and started reading. After the first paragraph, he was frowning. At the second, he was muttering to himself.

And by the third paragraph, the words were blurring beneath the red haze covering his vision.

Heart jumping, stomach twisting, temper spiking, Shane crumpled the edges of the paper in his fists and forced himself to keep reading.

Sex with the boss is never a smart move,

Tess wrote,

> but in my case, it was imbecilic. I've spent the
> last year or more writing about how hard it is
> to work with a man who never sees you as
> anything more than an especially fine tuned
> piece of office equipment. But now that Shane
> actually has seen me—naked of all things—
> the situation is completely untenable.

> So here's a word of warning for all of you
> assistants out there. When the boss smiles and
> says "Let's celebrate," remember that cele-
> brating usually means hangover.

> Or worse.

> For your own sakes, if the boss starts
> looking too good to you…run.

"Rachel," he muttered thickly, staring at the page
in front of him as if he still couldn't believe what
he'd read. "All this time, it's been her. All this time."

He swallowed hard, choking back the knot of
fury in his throat. When he thought he could speak
without growling, he snatched up the phone on his
desk and punched in a number.

"Circulation and archives."

"This is Shane Elliott."

"Yes, sir," the female voice snapped out, and he
could almost see the woman jerking to attention
in her chair.

"Get me a copy of every one of our magazines
that contains a Tess Tells All column."

"Oh, sir, I just love that column."

"Great," he muttered, thinking now about all of the people who'd read every word Rachel had ever written about him. Hell, people all over the *world* had been laughing at him for more than a year.

And he'd wanted to give the mysterious Tess a raise!

"I want those copies here in thirty minutes."

"Yes, sir."

Shane tossed the receiver back into the cradle, gave up on trying to rein in the temper nearly strangling him and started reading the most recent column again.

Ten

When Rachel came back from lunch, she was feeling a little better. She'd done a little Christmas shopping, wandered through the windy, cold streets and lost herself in the crowds.

Hard to keep feeling sorry for yourself when you're reminded that you're simply one cog in a very large wheel.

Now, back at *The Buzz,* she was simply determined to survive the rest of her two weeks notice and then move on with her life. Smiling at the people she passed, she headed right for her desk and noticed Shane's door standing open.

As she glanced inside, she saw that he'd been watching for her. And he didn't look happy.

"Everything okay?"

"Not really," he said, waving one hand at her. "Would you come in here please?"

A quick twist of apprehension tightened in her belly before she made a titanic attempt at smoothing it out. *Oh, God. He saw the column.*

Her brain raced, coming up with explanations, excuses, *anything.* She'd had a glass of wine at lunch, knowing that this confrontation would be headed her way. Now she wished she'd had two.

She paused long enough to deposit her purse in the bottom drawer of her desk, then steeling herself, walked into Shane's office and closed the door behind her. "What's going on?"

A brief, hard smile crossed his face. Standing up, he walked around the edge of his desk. Then folding his arms across his chest, he sat on the corner of the desk and watched her through narrowed eyes.

Rachel now knew how a rabbit felt staring down a snake. Fire flashed in his eyes and a twitch in his jaw told her he was gritting his teeth. No point in pretending ignorance any longer, she thought, and spoke right up. "You've seen the article."

"Not even going to try to deny it?"

"No."

"So you *are* Tess."

She smoothed the fall of her skirt, then clasped her hands together at her waist. Her fingers tightened until her knuckles went white. "Surprise."

"I can't believe this." He shook his head in disgust. "I don't even know whether to be insulted or flattered that you've been writing about me all these months."

"I didn't mean for you to find out like this."

"You mean," he corrected, pushing off the desk to stalk across the room toward her, "you didn't mean for me to find out at all."

"Well," she hedged, "yes."

He walked a slow circle around her and Rachel turned slowly, keeping her gaze fixed on him. "Did you enjoy watching me trying to find out ways to identify you? Did you get a laugh out of lying to everyone here? Lying to *me?*"

She huffed out a breath and mentally scrambled for the right thing to say. But she kept coming up empty. "I wasn't trying to lie to you, Shane."

"Ah, so that was just a happy side benefit."

"I don't know why you're making such a big deal about this," she said, deciding to go on the defensive. "You *loved* those columns."

"Yes," he snapped, coming to a fast stop. "When I thought they were written about some nameless, faceless *jerk*. I *don't* love finding out that *I'm* the jerk."

She held up one hand. "I never called you a jerk."

"You might as well have," he countered, spinning around and walking back to his desk. He picked up a thick manila file and waved it at her. "I've been going over all the old columns. And now that I think about it, I believe I'm more insulted than anything else. You made me look like a fool."

The knot of tension inside her started to loosen and

with it, came a burst of outrage. "I did not. All I did was write about the day-to-day job of working for you."

"And about the women I date."

In her own defense, she pointed out, "I wouldn't have had to write about that if you hadn't put *me* in charge of buying your make-up gifts, your break-up gifts. Ordering flowers. Making reservations for you and the Barbies, Bambis and Tawnys of the world."

"Tawny," he muttered. "That's her name."

"You're the one who dragged me into your social life, Shane, so you're hardly in a position to complain about it now, are you?"

"You're my assistant. Who the hell else would I ask to do all that stuff?"

She hitched one hip higher than the other, folded her arms under her breasts, cocked her head to stare at him and offered, "Oh, I don't know…*yourself?*"

He tossed the folder onto his desk and the columns inside scattered across the gleaming surface. "If you hated your job so much, why didn't you just quit?"

"I did," she reminded him.

"I mean before," he blustered, throwing both hands high. "If I'm such a bastard to work for, why did you stay this long?"

Rachel dropped the angry pose, walked forward and dropped down into one of the twin chairs opposite his desk. Looking up at him, she said, "You were never a bastard to work for. And I enjoyed my job. I just got…"

"Jealous?" he asked.

"No." She jumped to her feet again. "Not jealous, just—I don't even know what. I started writing those articles as a way to vent my frustration. And hey, apparently there are a lot of admins in the city who know just what I'm talking about."

"Yes, but—"

"You said yourself only last week that Tess Tells All is the most popular column in the magazine. You wanted to find her. To offer her—me—a weekly column. You wanted to give her a huge raise and bring her—me—on staff." She watched him and noted the relaxing of his jaw muscles and the tension dropping out of his squared shoulders. "So what's changed, Shane? Only the fact that you found out who Tess really is."

"That's plenty," he snapped.

"From your point of view, I guess so," she acknowledged. "But you have to admit that you laughed at my columns as hard as anyone else."

"That was before. Now..." He turned from her and walked to the windows. Staring out, he said, "You wrote about our nights together."

She swallowed hard and met his gaze when he looked over his shoulder at her. "Yes."

"Why?"

She shrugged and knew that wasn't an answer. But she wasn't sure she had one to give him. "I don't really know."

"I think I do," he said, turning back to face her again. "I think you wanted me to find out that you're Tess."

"Oh, I don't think that's it," she said, shaking her head slowly.

Shane walked toward her and noted that she took a half step back, as if trying to keep a safe distance between them. Wasn't going to work. He'd had time to think about this. Time to reread her columns with a clear eye.

"You wanted me to know, Rachel. Otherwise you never would have made the mistake of putting my name in the most recent article."

"That was a mistake."

"A Freudian slip."

"Oh, please," she said, backing away as he got closer.

"You wanted me to know because you don't want to quit your job. You don't want to leave *The Buzz*. You want your own column. You want to stay here. With me."

She laughed shortly. "I already turned in my resignation, Shane. And you accepted it."

"Reluctantly."

"Whatever. The point is, it's done."

She glanced around the room, keeping from looking at him, avoiding meeting his gaze. Shane actually enjoyed watching the usually unflappable Rachel display telltale signs of nervousness.

"No, it's not," he said. "I don't want you to quit, Rachel. I'm willing to offer you the same deal I was going to offer your alter ego."

Finally she looked at him. "You *want* me to keep writing about you?"

"No," he admitted. "But you're very talented. You're funny. And our readers love your columns. I'm guessing you could find something else to write about. Life in Manhattan. Interviews with other admins. Anything you want."

She thought about it for a long moment and Shane found himself wishing to hell he could read her mind, since nothing of what she was feeling was visible on her features.

"Well?" he prodded, anxious for her answer.

"Tempting," she admitted, backing up again. "But no. Thanks for the offer, but I'm leaving *The Buzz,* Shane."

Speaking up quickly, he offered her more money. Up to twice her present salary. Her eyes popped, but still she shook her head.

"It's not about the money and it's insulting to me that you're acting as though it is."

"You want to talk insulted?" he countered hotly. "You've made me a laughingstock all over New York for the last year."

Her lips thinned into a grim slash. "If you hadn't behaved like an idiot, I wouldn't have had so much ammunition."

"Oh, that's perfect."

"Look, Shane," she said, making a heroic attempt at controlling her temper. "You have the CEO position you wanted, but I can't be around you anymore. I just can't do it."

Disappointment gathered in his chest, warred with anger and tightened until he could hardly draw a breath. "Because of what happened between us."

"Partly," she said, nodding. "We can't just go back to our old working relationship, Shane. We can't pretend we didn't…"

Hell no, he couldn't pretend nothing had happened between them. Every waking minute she was there, in his mind. Every time he closed his eyes, he saw her. Felt her. Tasted her. She haunted him and he knew that even if she left, her memory would stay with him. Always.

"So let's just leave things as they are and part friends, all right?"

His gaze locked with hers, he tried to find some way to change her mind. To make her stay. He knew damn well that without her, he might never have won the competition with his siblings.

And he couldn't imagine trying to run all of EPH without Rachel's advice and common sense and humor. Damn it, she couldn't just walk out.

But she did.

She left him standing there staring at her back as she walked away.

The next couple of days, Rachel buried herself in the preparations for the big charity event that EPH sponsored every year. The rich, the famous and the infamous would gather in the ballroom atop the Waldorf-Astoria and donate enough money to keep several children's shelters running for a year.

She already had the flowers arranged for and the

caterers and band. Then she spent half the morning on the phone with security experts, lining up the extra guards they'd need on the doors. Running her finger down her list, she made several check marks and only frowned once.

Santa.

She still needed a Santa.

The one she'd used the year before was already booked and she couldn't hire just anyone to hand out gifts to children. Flipping through the phone book, she looked up several numbers for casting agents in the city. Somehow or other, she'd find the perfect Santa.

Her last job for EPH was going to come off perfectly even if she had to work herself to death to make sure of it.

When her phone rang, she reached for it automatically. "Shane Elliott's office."

"Ms. Adler?"

"Yes." Frowning, she sat back in her chair.

"This is Dylan Hightower at *Cherish* magazine."

"Oh." She straightened. *Cherish* was a celebrity homestyle magazine she'd applied to just last week. Good news. When she left EPH, she wanted to be able to go right into a new job.

"I wanted to call you and explain why we're unable to offer you a position."

She blinked, stunned. She was *perfect* for the job of executive assistant to the editor-in-chief. Her computer skills were excellent, matched by her organizational abilities and her work ethic. "I see."

"No, I don't believe you do," Hightower said

abruptly. "And frankly, I'm only calling to warn you that publishing is a very small business. Liars don't go undiscovered for long."

"I'm sorry?" Her stomach was spinning.

"You should apologize for wasting my time, Ms. Adler. I checked with your references and I have to say I was shocked when Shane Elliott told me the real story behind your leaving your present position."

"He did." Temper boiled and bubbled in the pit of her stomach and she was forced to take deep, even breaths to steady herself out. "What exactly did Mr. Elliott have to say, if you don't mind my asking?"

"Not at all. He informed me that you were quite possibly the worst assistant he's ever had. And the fact that you're not a team player and actually go out of your way to foment dissension in the ranks…" He paused for breath. "Let me just say that your reputation is less than stellar."

The edges of her vision went a blurry red. She could hardly speak she was so furious and it took all she had not to slam the phone down on Mr. Fabulous Hightower.

"I understand," she finally managed to say.

"I hope you do," he retorted and hung up.

Still clutching the phone, while a dial tone buzzed in her ear, Rachel shifted a look at Shane's closed door. Inhaling sharply, she slapped the phone into its cradle and stomped across the floor toward it. She didn't bother to knock, just shoved it open, slammed it shut behind her and advanced on her boss with blood in her eye.

"Rachel?"

"How *dare* you?" She slapped both hands on his desk and leaned in toward him. "How dare you submarine my chances at a new job."

"Now wait a—"

"Mr. Hightower just called to explain personally why he wouldn't be hiring me."

Shane's gaze snapped to one side and he scrubbed one hand across his face. "Oh."

"Yeah, *oh.*"

He looked at her again, but couldn't quite meet her eyes. "Now, Rachel—"

"I can't believe you did that, Shane. My God, are you really that petty?"

He jumped to his feet. The cityscape stretched out behind him, snow falling softly against the windows, blurring the edges of his silhouette. The silence in the office was profound.

"It wasn't that. It was—"

"What, Shane? What could possibly have been the motivator for you to tell people lies about me?" She pushed up from the desk, folded her arms across her chest and tapped the toe of her shoe against the carpet. "Four years I've worked for you and in all that time have I ever screwed up?"

"No."

"Fomented dissension in the ranks?"

"No."

"Then why?" she asked, shaking her head and

looking at him like she'd never seen him before. And indeed, this side of Shane was a mystery to her. Never before had she seen him so embarrassed. Ashamed.

He blew out a breath, shoved both hands into his pockets and rocked back on his heels. "I thought if I could slow down your job search you might change your mind about leaving."

"By lying about me. Amazing."

"A bad idea. I see that now."

"Well, congratulations," she snapped. "A breakthrough. You're finally willing to admit that not everything in the known universe is about Shane Elliott. Other people have their little lives and problems, too."

"Rachel, I'm sorry, I—"

"Forget it," she said, stepping back from his desk but keeping her eyes on him, as if expecting him to stab her in the back again. "It's a lesson learned, that's all. I'm sure I'll grow from the experience."

"Damn it…"

"You can have personnel send me my last check, Shane. I'm leaving now."

"You can't. You gave me two weeks notice."

She'd reached the door. Snaking her arm behind her, she turned the knob and pulled it open. "If you can lie," she said quietly, "then so can I. Goodbye, Shane."

Eleven

The dining room at The Tides, the Elliott family home, was elegant but warm. Deep burgundy walls, with cream colored trim and crown moldings gave it an old-world feeling. A polished to perfection walnut table that could easily sit twelve stood on a thick Oriental carpet. Original oil paintings dotted the walls and a hand carved buffet sat against the far wall.

When Patrick and Maeve Elliott hosted dinner parties, this room sparkled with fine crystal and fragile china. But Shane remembered all the years growing up in this house and he could almost hear the memory of his brothers' and sister's voices echoing off the walls.

The estate was palatial—seven thousand square feet of turn-of-the-century home, surrounded by five acres of meticulously cared for grounds, situated on a bluff overlooking the Atlantic Ocean in Long Island. And though the house could be intimidating to visitors, to the Elliott children it had simply been home. And a great place for spur-of-the-moment games of hide-and-seek.

The roar and hush of the nearby sea pulsed in the background, almost making the old house seem alive. Shane loved this house. But at the moment, he wished he were anywhere but there.

"Your Rachel is certainly a lovely girl," Maeve said, taking a tiny sip of white wine.

Shane snapped his mother a warning look. "She's not *my* Rachel and yes, she is."

"I sensed a bit of—"

"Mom."

He should have tried to get out of dinner tonight. But to do that, he'd have had to come up with a damn good explanation and at the moment, Shane just wasn't up to it.

Hell, even *he* couldn't believe how he'd sabotaged Rachel's attempts to leave EPH. It had seemed like a good idea at the time. Downplay her abilities, make her seem a little less employable and maybe she'd stay with him.

He hadn't meant to— Damn. Yes, he had. He *had* meant to screw things up for her. So what did that make him? A bastard? Or a desperate bastard?

Either way, he'd lost her.

She'd gathered up her things and walked out of the building right after leaving his office. And for the rest of the day, walking past her empty desk drove needles of guilt into his skull, making his head ache and his temper spike.

He could still see the expression on her face when she'd faced him down just a few hours ago. Shock, betrayal, fury. If he could have, he would have kicked his own ass. He never should have given into the temptation to sabotage her job search.

His own fault. He'd let Rachel become too important to him over the years. She'd become such a part of his day, he could barely imagine *not* having her there.

That thought irritated him more than a little and he scowled to himself.

"Fine, fine," Maeve said, having another sip before setting her glass down on the linen draped table. "Far be it from me to interfere in my children's lives."

Shane snorted a laugh and his mother's eyes narrowed on him.

"Well," she pointed out, "if you and your brothers and sisters would talk to me about what's bothering you, I wouldn't have to pry now would I?"

"Ah, so it's our fault."

"Darlin'," she said, a soft smile still curving her mouth, "I can plainly see that there's something bothering you. Won't you tell me?"

For a moment or two, he considered it. Just unloading on his mom. Then he thought about how

Maeve would react when she discovered what he'd done to Rachel and thought better of it.

"I spoke to Rachel this afternoon," his mother said into the silence.

"Really? About what?"

"The charity ball," Maeve reminded him. "She wanted to say that despite the fact she no longer worked for you, she would continue to oversee the preparations."

"Ah." Of course she'd do that. Rachel was the most responsible human being he'd ever known. She took her duties seriously and once she'd given herself up to a project, she never quit.

Not even when she had more than enough reason to.

"Idiot," he muttered, rubbing his eyes in an attempt to ease the headache pounding behind them.

"Aye," Maeve said, the Irish accent she'd never quite lost dancing in her tone, "apparently you are, dear. Would you like to explain to me why you've fired that lovely girl?"

"I didn't fire her."

"She quit?"

"Yes."

"Why?"

He slanted Maeve a look and wished he hadn't. He was thirty-eight years old, the newly crowned head of a Fortune 500 company and one steely glare from his mother could completely cow him.

Thankfully he was saved by an interruption.

"What're you two talking about?" Patrick asked

as he walked into the room, heels clicking on the marble floor, and took the chair at the head of the table.

"Not a thing, my love," Maeve said, patting his hand. But the look she sent Shane told him that this wasn't over.

"Hmm." Patrick wasn't convinced, but he was willing to let it go. Focusing his gaze on Shane, he asked, "Before dinner arrives, why don't you tell me what your plans are for the company?"

"Patrick," his wife said, "can't we have a single meal without discussing business?"

"No," Shane said quickly, eager to talk about anything but Rachel. If he could keep his mother's mind off of that subject, he just might be able to get through dinner and escape before she could corner him again. "It's fine. Actually I'd like to get Dad's opinion on a few things."

Maeve picked up her glass of wine and took a sip, focusing her gaze on her son. Shane pretended he didn't feel that hot stare and concentrated instead on his father.

The next week was a blur of activity.

Even though Rachel was now officially unemployed, she was busier than ever, coordinating the charity function. Keeping in touch with the event planner at the Waldorf, Rachel had her finger on every hot button.

Nothing was getting past her; she wouldn't allow it. If this was going to be her final task for EPH, it was going to be one that people would be talking about for years. She'd arranged for a ten-foot pine tree to be delivered and professionally decorated. There would be a champagne fountain, a chocolate bar and enough hors d'oeuvres to keep even the most famished guest satisfied.

Every table at the event would boast its own tiny tree, complete with twinkling lights, and garlands of holly and mistletoe would be wound around the perimeter of the elegant room.

This ball was going to be organized smoother than a military coup. There wouldn't be a single hiccup.

She took a bite of her maple scone and shifted a look out through the window of the coffeehouse at the street beyond. Dark clouds hovered over the city as if waiting for just the right moment to dump another few inches of snow on the already slushy streets. People were bundled up, colorful scarves wound tightly around their mouths and necks. And the wind whipped down the high-rise canyons, snatching up trash and twirling it through the air.

Made her cold just looking out at it. So she turned back to the paperwork spread out over the table in front of her and got back down to the business of running a charity event.

Her cell phone rang and Rachel rummaged in her oversized purse for it. A perky little tune played louder as she grabbed it, and a few of the patrons in the coffeehouse glared at her. "Hello?"

"Honey, how's it going?" Christina's voice came across in whispered concern.

Rachel leaned back in her chair, picked up her latte and took a drink. She'd only spoken to her friend once since leaving EPH and Rachel had really missed her. "It's going *great*."

"Uh-huh."

"Really." She put every ounce of conviction she possessed into her voice, but clearly it wasn't enough to convince Christina.

"Oh sure, I believe you."

"Fine," Rachel muttered, shooting a glare at a bearded man hunched over his laptop. What was up with him? He was allowed to type and clatter but she couldn't have a conversation? Honestly, some people.

Focusing on her friend, Rachel said, "I'm working myself to death to keep from thinking about Shane."

"That's what I figured. So if you're still so nuts about him, why'd you quit?"

"What other choice did I have?" she demanded a little too loudly and glared right back at the Beard. Lowering her voice, she said, "I couldn't stay there after—"

God, she couldn't even think about those nights with Shane. It was hard enough to lie there in her bed and remember him lying alongside her. To imagine the hush of his breath, the sweep of his hands on her body, the taste of his mouth on hers.

She took a gulp of hot coffee and burned her mouth. Good. Nice distraction.

"Okay," Christina said, "sex with the boss would make things a little…sticky."

"Yeah, just a touch. But it's more than that, too."

"You mean it's because you love him?"

Rachel winced. "Oh God. *Yes.* I do. And it's hopeless and pitiful and ridiculous and all of the above at once." She shook her head and trailed the tip of her index finger around the circumference of her coffee cup lid. "He's never going to see me like that. Never going to love me back. How could I stay there?"

"I guess you couldn't," Christina said on a sigh. "But I really miss you around here."

"Miss you, too. Heck, I miss my *job.* I was good at it, you know?"

"I know." There was a long pause and then Christina lowered her voice so much Rachel could scarcely hear her. "Would it help to know that since you've been gone, Shane's been miserable?"

Instantly Rachel cheered right up. "Really? His new admin isn't working out?"

"Doesn't have one."

"No way." Surprise made her voice a little louder again and this time Beard actually lifted his index finger to his mouth and warned, "Shhh." Rachel sneered at him.

Shane hadn't hired someone to take her place? Why not? She'd been gone a week. And heaven knew the man couldn't keep track of his own appointment schedule. He needed someone highly organized or he'd never get anything done. And that thought brought a small smile to her face.

"It's weird. Your desk sits there empty," Christina

said, "like the elephant at the cocktail party that nobody wants to talk about."

It shouldn't have made her feel better that Shane hadn't replaced her, but it did. She should be letting him go, getting on with the life she'd promised herself to find. But how could she, when every other minute Shane's face kept popping up into her mind?

"So who's doing all the work if he hasn't hired somebody?"

"No one. That seems to be the problem."

"Oh boy."

"Exactly. And he's not a happy camper these days. Shane's got every department head hopping. Jonathon even threatened to quit yesterday!"

"No, he didn't."

"Oh, yes, he did and Shane backed off quick. I mean, he's crabby, but he's not stupid. If he lost you *and* Jonathon, he'd really be up the proverbial creek. And to top it all off, Shane slams his office door so often, the doorjamb's coming loose."

For a moment or two, Rachel indulged herself, pretending that it was *her* he missed. But in reality she knew better. Right now he was angry because she hadn't fallen into line with his plans. He was feeling a little ashamed of himself for ruining Rachel's job opportunity and he was, no doubt, frustrated because his office life wasn't running as smoothly as usual.

"He'll survive," Rachel said firmly, "and so will I. I hope."

"You hang in there, honey," Christina said. "How about you and I meet for dinner tonight?"

"I'd really love to," Rachel assured her, "but I can't. I have to go to my folks' house for the annual What's Wrong with Rachel holiday discussion."

"Man. You just can't catch a break, can you?"

Actually she *did* catch a small break.

Another storm was rushing toward the city, so to avoid having to drive in a blizzard Rachel made her excuses and left her parents' house early.

Not nearly early enough, though.

She flipped on the rental car radio and tuned it to a soft rock station. The windshield wipers slapped against the glass, keeping time with the rhythm of the song. Nearly hypnotized, Rachel started talking to herself, more to stay alert than anything else.

"A podiatrist. *This* is the dream doctor Mom wants me to hook up with?" Okay, he was a perfectly nice man and not too bad looking in that "probably has back hair" kind of way. But could the man *be* more boring?

"Feet. That's all he talked about all night—feet." Rachel was willing to admit that in the grand scheme of things, feet were a fairly important body part. After all, they made walking a lot easier. But she now knew way more than she'd ever wanted to know about corns, blisters, calluses and warts.

"That's it, Mom," she swore and slapped one hand against the steering wheel. "No more fix-ups. I absolutely refuse."

Her cell phone rang and she reached one handed into her purse, on the passenger seat. Keeping her eyes on the road, she didn't even look at the screen, just opened the phone and said, "Hello?"

"Rachel."

Chills swept up and down her spine, ran along her arms, across her knuckles and back up to swirl in a happy little clog dance in the middle of her chest. God, would the sound of his voice always have that effect on her? "Hello, Shane."

He smiled at the sound of her voice, even though it was less than welcoming. Ever since leaving his parents' house, Shane'd been thinking about Rachel. Hell, he hadn't been able to get his mind off of her all week. Every time he passed her empty desk, he was reminded again of what an idiot he was.

The nights were the worst, though. He glanced around his apartment and found no pleasure in the stark, designer furnishings. White couches, hardwood floors and a lot of glass and chrome, much like the offices at *The Buzz.* His home had all the warmth of a dentist's office. And, at the moment, about the same appeal.

He kept remembering being at Rachel's place. A small, cozy place that she'd made warm and friendly. He could see her, all curled up in one corner of the couch, her blond hair lying loose in soft waves. He heard her laughter and remembered the passion in her eyes.

He couldn't stop thinking about carrying her into her bedroom and how she'd looked in the pale glow of the streetlight shining through the window. He couldn't seem to sleep without tasting her again, reaching for her, like a blind man fumbling for a life rope he knows is there, but can't find.

During the last week, he'd been forced to admit to himself just how important Rachel really was to him. And the question Gannon had asked him a couple of weeks ago kept replaying over and over again in his mind.

Do you love Rachel?

He'd spent so many years avoiding that particular word that now a part of him recoiled even at the thought of it. But the more he missed Rachel, the more he was forced to acknowledge that maybe love had sneaked up on him.

Maybe.

But how was a man supposed to *know?*

The only way he could think of was to get Rachel to come back to work at *The Buzz,* so that they could spend more time together. And then maybe what he was feeling would start to make sense to him.

He walked across the living room of his spacious apartment overlooking Central Park and stopped opposite the terrace doors. Behind him, a fire roared in the hearth, in front of him, a storm was blowing in off the Atlantic, threatening to shut the city down this time.

And he was oblivious to everything but the woman on the other end of the line. He held the phone to his ear in a white-knuckled grip and asked, "Is this a bad time, Rachel?"

"Actually…"

He'd only said that to be polite, so he spoke up

fast. Couldn't risk her hanging up on him. He figured it was best if he went straight to the point. "Rachel, you've gotta come back to work."

"What?"

"I mean it. The place is falling apart, nothing's getting done."

What he didn't say was that it wasn't just work that concerned him. The real problem was *him*. He couldn't think anymore. Without seeing Rachel every damn day, it was like part of his life—the most important part—was gone.

"Not my problem anymore."

He slapped one hand on the icy glass of the French doors and tried to keep his voice calm, steady, without betraying any of the panic he was beginning to feel. It wasn't easy. "Damn it, Rachel, without you there, nothing works right. Nothing is what it should be. I need you, Rachel."

For some reason, something his father had said to him just a couple of weeks ago came flying back into his brain. *Winning doesn't mean a damn thing if you've got nothing to show for it but the victory.*

The old man was right, he thought. Without Rachel to share things with, the victory he'd won over his brothers and sister was an empty one.

There was a long pause where all he heard was a radio playing softly. He stared out at the swirling snow and noted the lamps and the blazing fire behind him reflected in the glass. He waited what seemed like forever for her answer and when it finally came, it wasn't what he wanted to hear.

"You don't need *me,* Shane," she said, her voice sounding sad and weary. "I really wish you did. But what you need is a good admin. There are plenty of them in New York. Find one."

"Rachel, wait—"

"Goodbye, Shane."

Twelve

She wasn't coming back.

Shane scrubbed both hands across his face and blew out a shaky breath. He looked around his office and tried to find the excitement, the old sense of pride being here used to give him. But there was nothing.

Nothing at all.

The work went on.

The world went on.

But nothing was the same.

Rachel was gone.

And he didn't know how to fix it.

When the phone rang, he almost ignored it. God knew he was in no mood to talk to anyone. But the shrill rings sliced into his head, accentuating the headache already pounding behind his eyes. So he grabbed it and snarled a greeting.

"Well, Merry Christmas to you, too," a familiar female voice said.

"Fin." He sighed, plopped down into his desk chair and spun around so that he was facing the windows and the cold, dark world beyond the glass. Outside, the sky was gray and heavy. New York had been getting quite the winter this year and it looked as if it was going to keep right on snowing through Christmas.

Christmas. Only about ten days away and he still didn't have any shopping done. Another example of just how much he missed Rachel. She'd have made damn sure he got out to the stores.

Pitiful, he thought. He couldn't even Christmas shop without Rachel in his life.

Just pitiful.

"So," he said, "you coming home for Christmas?"

"I don't think so," Fin answered. "I sort of want to start our own traditions this year. But I'll definitely be there for the New Year's party."

Disappointment flared briefly to life inside him. He hadn't realized how much he'd been looking forward to seeing his sister again.

Shaking his head, he forced a smile into his voice and asked, "So how's life in the Wild, Wild West?"

Fin laughed again and Shane saw her in his mind. His twin. His best friend. Like a younger version of their mother, Fin was short and slender with auburn hair, green eyes and a few gold freckles across her nose. Her smile could light up a room and he was grateful that lately, his twin had had so much to smile about.

Fin might be living on a ranch in Colorado these days, but clearly their connection was still strong. She'd chosen just the right time to call him.

"You really need to get out of Manhattan more often, Shane," she said, still chuckling. "You know, we really don't have gunfights in the center of town and desperadoes hardly ever hold up the stagecoach anymore."

"Cute," he said, nodding, "and the ranch was a great place to visit but I think the West Village is about as west as I really want to go."

His sister sighed a little. "I know you're not the out-doorsy type, Shane, but I know you enjoyed yourself."

The Silver Moon ranch, just outside Colorado Springs, was mainly a cattle ranch, but according to Fin, her new husband ran quite a few horses, too. Enough to make her happy anyway.

And it wasn't as if his city born and bred sister was roughing it. She and her husband, Travis Clayton, lived in a huge, two-story log home, sur-rounded by tall pines and open spaces. Shane had seen for himself how happy she was there. And that was good enough for him.

"I did. And I'll come back," he promised. "This spring. In the meantime, how're you feeling?"

"Good," she said, a little less enthusiastically. "I could live without the morning sickness, but other-wise, I feel great."

Shane smiled. "I'm glad. And damn, it's good to hear your voice."

"Yeah," she said wryly, "you sound thrilled."

"Been a bad couple of weeks," he admitted, leaning his head against the chair back.

"Not the way I hear it," she said. "You made it, Shane. You're the new CEO. This is a good thing."

Should have been, he told himself. Now it didn't mean a thing to him. How could it when the woman who'd helped him win the damn thing was gone?

His silence must have told her there was something wrong.

"So do you want to tell me what's going on?" she asked.

"I wouldn't know where to start," he admitted.

"Most people say start at the beginning," Fin said and he heard the smile in her voice. "I say start with what's upsetting you and work backward."

"Upset?" he repeated. "Small word for what I'm feeling." Hell. What *was* he feeling? He couldn't ever remember experiencing this kind of emotion. The feeling that his chest was too tight. That his heart was empty.

That he might never be *warm* again.

"Talk to me, Shane."

"It's Rachel," he blurted. "She's gone."

"What do you mean gone?"

He frowned at the phone. "How many things could I mean?"

"She quit?"

"Yeah." He bit the word off and tasted the bitterness of defeat.

"Why?"

He rubbed his mouth, closed his eyes and said, "Because I'm an idiot."

Fin chuckled. "She's known that for a long time, but she just now quit, so what else happened?"

"We—" He caught himself and shook his head. "None of your business, Fin."

"Well, *yahoo*," she crowed. "It's about time."

"What?"

"You slept with her."

"Like I said, none of your business." And why was his twin, the one person in the world who should be on his side at all damn times, so excited by his misery?

"So did you tell her you love her?"

He sat up like a shot and noticed the horrified expression on his reflection in the windowpane. "Who said anything about love?"

"Oh, Shane, I love you, but you really *are* an idiot."

"Thanks for calling," he snapped.

"For Pete's sake, everyone but you has known for at least a year that Rachel's nuts about you."

"What?" If that was true, why hadn't he known about it? Why hadn't someone told him? Hell, why hadn't he *noticed?*

"And you feel the same way."

He shook his head firmly, decisively. "I'm not in love."

"Really?" his sister prompted. "Then why don't

you tell me how you're feeling now that Rachel's gone?"

He scowled and his reflection glared back at him.

"Be honest," she said and her voice softened in sympathy.

"I feel like hell," he finally said, admitting what he'd been keeping inside for too long. "Nothing feels right without her here. Nothing's working. I can't work. Can't think. Can't sleep. Damn it, Fin, I wasn't looking for this."

"No, you weren't. You just got lucky."

"I'm *lucky* to feel this bad?"

"No, Shane," she said on an impatient sigh. "You're lucky to have the chance at something amazing. Most people never find what you have. Don't blow it."

He shook his head, as if he were going to try to deny his sister's words. But he couldn't. "I already *have* blown it. Fin, she won't talk to me. Won't see me."

"Then it's up to you to find a way to make it happen."

"Easier said than done."

"Nobody said it would be easy. Nothing worth having comes easily, Shane." A long pause and then her voice dipped even lower. "Trust me on this one. I know."

Fin had gone through so much in her life to reach the happiness she'd finally found, he knew she was speaking from experience. But just because she and Travis had found each other didn't mean that he and Rachel were destined to find the same thing.

Did it?

Was Fin right?

Was it all so simple after all?

Was this overpowering emotion nearly choking him *love?*

"Shane," Fin said quietly, and he focused on the sound of her voice, "for too long, I was living only for the company. I forgot about actually having a life. But now, I've got a wonderful life, with a man who loves me. I've found my daughter and I have a new chance at being a mom."

"I know and I'm glad for you—"

"I want the same kind of happiness for you, Shane," she said, interrupting him neatly. "Don't let Rachel get away. Don't miss your chance at love."

When he finally hung up with Fin, Shane was thoughtful. Everything she'd said played over and over again in his mind, as if the words were on a permanent loop. Love. Rachel. Chance at happiness.

The silence in his office pushed him to leave it. As he wandered through the deserted hallways of *The Buzz,* his footsteps echoing in the quiet, he felt the underlying pulse of the business his father had built. Everything that he himself was now responsible for. And weirdly, he felt both fulfilled and empty.

This place was where he belonged, but the woman who belonged *with* him wasn't there.

And without Rachel, he knew suddenly, none of this was worth a damn. Fin was right. If he didn't act quickly, do *something* to convince Rachel to take a chance on him again, he'd end up just like his father—a lonely man with more regrets than anyone had a right to.

Patrick Elliott loved his wife madly, but he'd so buried himself in the business he'd created, that he'd missed much of the life they could have had. He'd been a stranger to his children and a phantom presence in his own house.

Shane didn't want the same kind of life.

He didn't want to be a man whose only happiness lay in the profit margins of his business. He wanted to be happy. To love and *be* loved.

He wanted Rachel.

Now, all he had to do was convince her that she still wanted *him*.

The Waldorf-Astoria hotel was decked out in all its grandeur for the Elliott Charity Gala. Towering floral centerpieces sat atop gleaming tables that lined the marble foyer where elegantly dressed attendees mingled, enjoying appetizers and champagne.

Crystal chandeliers shimmered with quiet light and led the guests along the marble hallway toward the elevators that would take them to the grand ballroom. Upstairs, the long, narrow room was ablaze with strings of white lights. A DJ stood along one wall, playing a selection of Christmas music that had feet tapping and a few couples twirling on the dance floor.

In one corner of the room, a gigantic blue spruce tree stood proudly, its limbs bowing under the weight of lights and ornaments. At its feet were dozens of gaily wrapped packages awaiting the crowd of children here representing those this fundraiser would be assisting.

Rachel smiled and nodded to those she passed as she listened with half an ear to the voices coming across the earpiece/microphone she wore. Keeping everything running smoothly was enough of a task that she didn't really have time to think about Shane. Or the fact that he wasn't there.

She'd missed him desperately the last week or so. Missed going into work every day and seeing him. Missed teasing him and hearing him laugh. Missed working with him and sharing the victories and defeats of running *The Buzz*.

And every night, alone in her bed, she missed the feel of his arms around her. Missed the sound of his breath in the darkness and the heated touch of his hands on her body.

She closed her eyes and swayed slightly under the onslaught of memories rushing through her. Rachel's heart ached as her gaze swept the crowd, searching for the one man she most longed to see. But he wasn't there and in the ocean of people, she might as well have been alone.

Two hours later, the DJ began playing "Here Comes Santa Claus," and the gathered children erupted in excited cheers.

A voice in Rachel's ear said, "Santa's here, and hey, it's a good one."

"Excellent," she answered and followed the

crowd as the people slowly moved toward the decorated Christmas tree and the "throne" that had been
set up for Santa.

Then the man himself stepped out from behind a
panel of velvet curtains and paused midstage for a
hearty belly laugh. His voice rolled out across the
room and sent a chill straight up Rachel's spine.

Her heartbeat quickened and her mouth went dry
as her gaze locked on the tall man in the red velvet
suit. The red hat, white wig and beard, bushy
eyebrows and rectangular glasses perched low on his
nose did a good job of disguising his true identity.

But Rachel would have known him anywhere.

Shane.

She wove through the crowd, excusing herself,
apologizing, but never stopping. Her gaze on Santa,
she headed straight for him. And halfway there, his
gaze found hers. She felt the power of his stare slam
into her and for the first time in more than a week,
she felt wholly, completely alive again.

"Merry Christmas," Santa shouted, his gaze still
on Rachel.

The children shrieked and clapped and the
gathered adults got into the spirit of the thing, too.
Women in diamonds, men in designer tuxes smiled
along with the kids, enjoying the thrill of the moment.

Rachel stopped alongside Santa and looked up
into Shane's beautiful green eyes. She didn't want
to make too much of his being here. Of his playing
Santa. Of the quickening jolt of her heartbeat.

But how could she not?

How could she not hope that somehow, someway, they might find each other in the magic of this night?

"Santa's got some work to do," Shane whispered, "but once the presents are distributed, you and I have to talk."

"Shane…"

His eyes actually twinkled. *"Santa."*

She nodded even as one of the kids moved in close and started tugging at her hand. "After, Santa."

Shane grinned and immediately bent down to scoop up the little girl who was staring at him as if he held the answers to all of the universe's questions. Perching her on his hip, he tapped her nose with the tip of one finger and said, "Now, let's see what Santa's got especially for you!"

For an hour, Rachel worked side by side with Shane. His laughter rang out and inspired hers. The kids were awed and touched and thrilled with the gifts the Elliott foundation had purchased specifically for them. The real magic of Christmas hummed in the air as the crowd began singing along with the carols pouring from the stereo.

Outside, the snow started again and turned the ballroom into a picture postcard. And when the last of the children's wishes had been satisfied, Santa took Rachel's hand and pulled her backstage.

"You were wonderful tonight," she said, taking a cautious step back from him even as her heart urged her to move in closer. "The children loved you."

Shane pulled off the hat, wig and beard, then carefully took off his glasses and set them aside before turning to Rachel. "I've never had so much fun," he admitted. "And it's all because of you."

"What?"

"You, Rachel," he said, reaching for her, dropping his hands onto her shoulders and pulling her slowly toward him. "I played Santa tonight because I knew you'd be here. Knew you'd like it. And I hoped you'd give me a chance to say what I should have said a long time ago."

"Shane…" Her throat felt incredibly tight. As if air were just too thick to penetrate it.

"Just listen," he said quickly. "Please."

Rachel nodded because she simply couldn't speak. She locked her knees to keep herself upright and stared into his beautiful eyes.

"I miss you, Rachel," he said, his voice gruff, raw. "I miss seeing you every day. Miss hearing you laugh. Miss the way you nag me into doing what needs doing."

She found her voice at that. "I don't nag, I—"

"You do," he interrupted, "and I need it, God knows. Nothing is right with me, Rachel. Since you left, there's no light. There's no laughter. There's no…anything."

"I miss you, too, but—"

"No," he said quickly, pulling her even closer, tipping her head back until she was staring straight up into his eyes. "No buts, Rachel. Just the simple truth. Without you in my life, I've got nothing worth having."

She swallowed hard and let the tears crowding her eyes begin to fall.

"I love you, Rachel," he said, his fingers digging into her arms as if holding on to her meant life itself. "I think maybe I've always loved you. I just never knew it until you were gone." He bent his head, kissed her gently, lightly, then said, "You're everything to me, Rachel. You make me want to be a better man. A man who deserves you."

Her heart thundering in her chest, Rachel could hardly believe she was hearing him say all the things she'd dreamed of hearing. Her soul lit up like Christmas morning and hope for a future filled with love swept through her.

"If you let me," he said, hurrying on as if unwilling to stop talking long enough to hear her answer, "I'll spend the rest of our lives proving to you just how much I love you."

"What are you saying?" The words squeaked out of her throat. She was pretty sure what he was getting at, but she wanted no mistakes. No misunderstandings. Not about this.

"I'm proposing, Rachel!" He dragged her tightly against him and wrapped his arms around her, holding her in place. "For God's sake, haven't you been listening?"

Rachel laughed and nodded. "Yeah. I really have. But I don't think I've heard an actual question yet."

He gave her a brief smile. "I'm getting to it. This isn't easy for a man, you know. What if the woman you're asking says no?"

She smiled back at him. "Just a chance you're going to have to take, I guess."

"Well," Shane said, "a very wise woman I know told me recently that nothing worth having comes easily."

"I like her already," Rachel said, loving the feel of Shane's arms around her, there in the dark. From the room beyond, Christmas music drifted on the air and conversations came muted, as if from a distant planet.

"Yeah," he said, "me, too. But this is about us."

"Us," Rachel echoed. "I like the sound of that, too."

"Glad to hear it," Shane said, lifting one hand to smooth her hair back from her forehead. "Marry me, Rachel. Let me marry you."

"Yes."

His smile was quick and broad. "Just like that?"

"Just like that," she said, nodding. "Although, I'm not going to work for you anymore."

His smile faded abruptly. "Why the hell not?"

"Because," she said, "I'm going back to school. I always wanted to be a teacher. I think I'd be a good one."

"I think you'd be a great teacher," Shane said, dipping his head for another quick taste of her. "I'll miss having you at the office, but as long as you come home to me every night, I'll be a happy man."

"I do love you, Santa," she said, going up on her toes to meet him for another kiss.

His glued-on, bushy white eyebrows wiggled expressively over his twinkling green eyes. "Then how about a sleigh ride?"

Epilogue

The tree was still up, the garlands and lights still twining around the great room at The Tides. And with all of the Elliotts gathered at the family home for New Year's, the noise level was pretty impressive.

Shane wandered through the crowd, listening to snatches of conversation and smiling at the sudden bursts of laughter that shot up and flavored the air. He glanced across the room, caught Rachel's eye and felt again the punch of sheer joy that was a constant companion these days. With Rachel's love he could do anything. Face anything. And he looked forward to a future of loving her and the children they were already trying for.

The stereo was suddenly turned off and each of

the gathered Elliotts turned to look at the older man standing beside the roaring fire in the hearth.

"I think it's time for a speech," Patrick Elliott announced, lifting a glass of champagne to his family.

"Now, Patrick," his wife chided, "'tis no time for one of your long talks. The family's here, we should be celebratin'."

Shane watched as his father dropped an arm around his wife's shoulders and pulled her close.

"You're right, Maeve," Patrick said, "as always. But, the idea was for Shane to give the speech. As the new CEO of EPH, it's only fitting."

Around him, applause erupted and Shane grinned. Gannon slapped him on the back and gave him a shove toward the front of the room. Erika held their baby daughter as if she were made of spun glass and smiled up at her husband.

Tag had his fiancée, Renee, trapped under a ball of mistletoe and the lovely woman showed no signs of trying to escape. Michael stood beside the chair where his wife, Karen, practically glowing with her very short hair, sat enjoying the fun.

Shane kept walking, stopping long enough to snag Rachel's hand and drag her along with him. He grinned at Summer and her rock star Zeke, huddled with Scarlet and John, no doubt planning the double wedding that Maeve was already fretting over.

Outside the living room, the night was cold and moonlit, pale silvery light glancing off the mounds of snow, illuminating the grounds. Inside, warmth filled the gathered Elliotts and touched Shane more deeply than ever before.

Fin lifted a glass to him and gave him a wink. He grinned at her and her husband, Travis, who'd flown in from Colorado with Bridget and her husband, Mac, just for this traditional party. In a corner of the room, Daniel and Amanda were cuddling, ignoring everyone else. And to round out the crowd, Jessie and her husband, Cade, were talking with Liam and his fiancée, Aubrey, about their upcoming wedding at their Napa winery. Collen and Misty were cuddled up together, as if they were alone on an island. And Bryan and Lucy were kissing under the mistletoe. The family was together and happy. A great start to a New Year.

Finally, though, Shane was at the head of the room and as his parents stepped to one side, he pulled Rachel close against him. His heart swelled as she leaned into him.

"I'm a lucky man," he said, lifting his glass to the faces turned toward him. "I found the woman I was meant to love and the work I was meant to do."

"Hear, hear!" Gannon shouted and was quickly shushed by Erika.

"But," Shane continued, looking from one beloved face to another, "I think this year we all got lucky. When Dad started his little contest, I thought he was trying to drive a wedge between us." Shane glanced at his father and smiled. "I should have known better."

Patrick smiled and kissed Maeve.

Renee gave Tag a friendly slap and stepped out from under the mistletoe to listen.

"The Elliotts have come together this year," Shane said, lifting his champagne glass even higher. "We've rediscovered our family ties and forged the bonds that connect us one to the other, even tighter than they were before. We've passed our own tests, we've faced our fears…" He paused to nod at Michael and Karen. "And we've come out the other side. We've found love and we've found each other."

Liam whistled and Fin applauded.

"Old wrongs have been righted," Shane went on, with a nod at Fin and Jessie. "And the future stretching out in front of us looks bright."

"Well said," Patrick called out.

"To the Elliotts," Shane shouted, "together, we're invincible!"

And as the family celebrated, Shane pulled the love of his life into the circle of his arms. Together, they shared a kiss that promised a future filled with all the love and hope anyone could ask for.

* * * * *

A new dynasty launches next month in Silhouette Desire. Don't miss DAKOTA FORTUNES, *starting off with Peggy Moreland's* MERGER OF FORTUNES *on sale in January.*

*Experience entertaining women's fiction for
every woman who has wondered
"what's next?" in their lives.
Turn the page for a sneak preview
of a new book from Harlequin NEXT,
WHY IS MURDER ON THE MENU, ANYWAY?
by Stevi Mittman*

On sale December 26, wherever books are sold.

Design Tip of the Day

Ambience is everything. Imagine eating a foie gras at a luncheonette counter or a side of cole-slaw at Le Cirque. It's not a matter of food but one of atmosphere. Remember that when planning your dining room design.
—Tips from *Teddi.com*

"Now that's the kind of man you should be looking for," my mother, the self-appointed keeper of my shelf-life stamp, says. She points with her fork at a man in the corner of the Steak-Out Restaurant, a dive I've just been hired to redecorate. Making this restaurant look four-star will be hard, but not half as hard as getting through lunch without strangling the woman across the table from me. "*He* would make a good husband."

"Oh, you can tell that from across the room?" I ask, wondering how it is she can forget that when we had trouble getting rid of my last husband, she shot him. "Besides being ten minutes away from death if he actually eats all that steak, he's twenty years too old for me and—shallow woman that I am—twenty pounds too heavy. Besides, I am *so* not looking for another husband here. I'm looking to design a new image for this place, looking for some sense of ambience, some feeling, something I can build a proposal on for them."

My mother studies the man in the corner, tilting her head, the better to gauge his age, I suppose. I think she's grimacing, but with all the Botox and Restylane injected into that face, it's hard to tell. She takes another bite of her steak salad, chews slowly so that I don't miss the fact that the steak is a poor cut and tougher than it should be. "You're concentrating on the wrong kind of proposal," she says finally. "Just look at this place, Teddi. It's a dive. There are hardly any other diners. What does *that* tell you about the food?"

"That they cater to a dinner crowd and it's lunchtime," I tell her.

I don't know what I was thinking bringing her here with me. I suppose I thought it would be better than eating alone. There really are days when my common sense goes on vacation. Clearly, this is one of them. I mean, really, did I not resolve less than three weeks ago that I would not let my mother get to me anymore?

What good are New Year's resolutions, anyway?

Mario approaches the man's table and my mother studies him while they converse. Eventually Mario leaves the table with a huff, after which the diner glances up and meets my mother's gaze. I think she's smiling at him. That or she's got indigestion. They size each other up.

I concentrate on making sketches in my notebook and try to ignore the fact that my mother is flirting. At nearly seventy, she's developed an unhealthy interest in members of the opposite sex to whom she isn't married.

According to my father, who has broken the TMI rule and given me Too Much Information, she has no interest in sex with him. Better, I suppose, to be clued in on what they aren't doing in the bedroom than have to hear what they might be doing.

"He's not so old," my mother says, noticing that I have barely touched the Chinese chicken salad she warned me not to get. "He's got about as many years on you as you have on your little cop friend."

She does this to make me crazy. I know it, but it works all the same. "Drew Scoones is not my little 'friend.' He's a detective with whom I—"

"Screwed around," my mother says. I must look shocked, because my mother laughs at me and asks if I think she doesn't know the "lingo."

What I thought she didn't know was that Drew and I actually tangled in the sheets. And, since it's possible she's just fishing, I sidestep the issue and tell her that Drew is just a couple of years younger than me and that I don't need reminding. I dig into my salad with renewed vigor, determined to show my mother that Chinese chicken salad in a steak place was not the stupid choice it's proving to be.

After a few more minutes of my picking at the wilted leaves on my plate, the man my mother has me nearly engaged to pays his bill and heads past us toward the back of the restaurant. I watch my mother take in his shoes, his suit and the diamond pinkie ring that seems to be cutting off the circulation in his little finger.

"Such nice hands," she says after the man is out of sight. "Manicured." She and I both stare at my hands. I have two popped acrylics that are being held on at weird angles by bandages. My cuticles are ragged and there's marker decorating my right hand from measuring carelessly when I did a drawing for a customer.

Twenty minutes later she's disappointed that he managed to leave the restaurant without our noticing. He will join the list of the ones I let get away. I will hear about him twenty years from now when—according to my mother—my children will be grown and I will still be single, living pathetically alone with several dogs and cats.

After my ex, that sounds good to me.

The waitress tells us that our meal has been taken care of by the management and, after thanking Mario, the owner, complimenting him on the wonderful meal and assuring him that once I have redecorated his place people will be flocking here in droves (I actually use those words and ignore my mother when she rolls her eyes), my mother and I head for the restroom.

My father—unfortunately not with us today— has the patience of a saint. He got it over the years of living with my mother. She, perhaps as a result, figures he has the patience for both of them, and feels justified having none. For her, no rules apply, and a little thing like a picture of a man on the door to a public restroom is certainly no barrier to using the john. In all fairness, it does seem silly to stand and wait for the ladies' room if no one is using the men's room.

Still, it's the idea that rules don't apply to her, signs don't apply to her, conventions don't apply to her. She knocks on the door to the men's room. When no one answers she gestures to me to go in ahead. I tell her that I can certainly wait for the ladies' room to be free and she shrugs and goes in herself.

Not a minute later there is a bloodcurdling scream from behind the men's room door.

"Mom!" I yell. "Are you all right?"

Mario comes running over, the waitress on his heels. Two customers head our way while my mother continues to scream.

I try the door, but it is locked. I yell for her to open it and she fumbles with the knob. When she finally manages to unlock and open it, she is white behind her two streaks of blush, but she is on her feet and appears shaken but not stirred.

"What happened?" I ask her. So do Mario and the waitress and the few customers who have migrated to the back of the place.

She points toward the bathroom and I go in, thinking it serves her right for using the men's room. But I see nothing amiss.

She gestures toward the stall, and, like any self-respecting and suspicious woman, I poke the door open with one finger, expecting the worst.

What I find is worse than the worst.

The husband my mother picked out for me is sitting on the toilet. His pants are puddled around his ankles, his hands are hanging at his sides. Pinned to his chest is some sort of Health Department certificate.

Oh, and there is a large, round, bloodless bullet hole between his eyes.

Four Nassau County police officers are securing the area, waiting for the detectives and crime scene personnel to show up. They are trying, though not very hard, to comfort my mother, who in another era would be considered to be suffering from the vapors. Less tactful in the twenty-first century, I'd say she was losing it. That is, if I didn't know her better, know she was milking it for everything it was worth.

My mother loves attention. As it begins to flag, she swoons and claims to feel faint. Despite four No Smoking signs, my mother insists it's all right for her to light up because, after all, she's in shock. Not to mention that signs, as we know, don't apply to her.

When asked not to smoke, she collapses mournfully in a chair and lets her head loll to the side, all without mussing her hair.

Eventually, the detectives show up to find the four patrolmen all circled around her, debating whether to administer CPR, smelling salts or simply call the paramedics. I, however, know just what will snap her to attention.

"Detective Scoones," I say loudly. My mother parts the sea of cops.

"We have to stop meeting like this," he says lightly to me, but I can feel him checking me over with his eyes, making sure I'm all right while pretending not to care.

"What have you got in those pants?" my mother asks him, coming to her feet and staring at his crotch accusingly. *"Baydar?* Everywhere we Bayers are, you turn up. You don't expect me to buy that this is a coincidence, I hope."

Drew tells my mother that it's nice to see her, too, and asks if it's his fault that her daughter seems to attract disasters.

Charming to be made to feel like the bearer of a plague.

He asks how I am.

"Just peachy," I tell him. "I seem to be making a habit of finding dead bodies, my mother is driving me crazy and the catering hall I booked two freakin' years ago for Dana's bat mitzvah has just been shut down by the Board of Health!"

"Glad to see your luck's finally changing," he

says, giving me a quick squeeze around the shoulders before turning his attention to the patrolmen, asking what they've got, whether they've taken any statements, moved anything, all the sort of stuff you see on TV, without any of the drama. That is, if you don't count my mother's threats to faint every few minutes when she senses no one's paying attention to her.

Mario tells his waitstaff to bring everyone espresso, which I decline because I'm wired enough. Drew pulls him aside and a minute later I'm handed a cup of coffee that smells divinely of Kahlúa.

The man knows me well. Too well.

His partner, whom I've met once or twice, says he'll interview the kitchen staff. Drew asks Mario if he minds if he takes statements from the patrons first and gets to him and the waitstaff afterward.

"No, no," Mario tells him. "Do the patrons first." Drew raises his eyebrow at me like he wants to know if I get the double entendre. I try to look bored.

"What is it with you and murder victims?" he asks me when we sit down at a table in the corner.

I search them out so that I can see you again, I almost say, but I'm afraid it will sound desperate instead of sarcastic.

My mother, lighting up and daring him with a look to tell her not to, reminds him that *she* was the one to find the body.

Drew asks what happened *this time*. My mother tells him how the man in the john was "taken" with me, couldn't take his eyes off me and blatantly flirted with both of us. To his credit, Drew doesn't laugh, but his smirk is undeniable to the trained eye. And I've had my eye trained on him for nearly a year now.

"While he was noticing you," he asks me, "did *you* notice anything about him? Was he waiting for anyone? Watching for anything?"

I tell him that he didn't appear to be waiting or watching. That he made no phone calls, was fairly intent on eating and did, indeed, flirt with my mother. This last bit Drew takes with a grain of salt, which was the way it was intended.

"And he had a short conversation with Mario," I tell him. "I think he might have been unhappy with the food, though he didn't send it back."

Drew asks what makes me think he was dissatisfied, and I tell him that the discussion seemed acrimonious and that Mario looked distressed when he left the table. Drew makes a note and says he'll look into it and asks about anyone else in the restaurant. Did I see anyone who didn't seem to belong, anyone who was watching the victim, anyone looking suspicious?

"Besides my mother?" I ask him, and Mom huffs and blows her cigarette smoke in my direction.

I tell him that there were several deliveries, the kitchen staff going in and out the back door to grab a smoke. He stops me and asks what I was doing checking out the back door of the restaurant.

Proudly—because, while he was off forgetting me, dropping by only once in a while to say hi to Jesse, my son, or drop something by for one of my daughters that he thought they might like, I was getting on with my life—I tell him that I'm decorating the place.

He looks genuinely impressed. "Commercial customers? That's great," he says. Okay, that's what he *ought* to say. What he actually says is "Whatever pays the bills."

"Howard Rosen, the famous restaurant critic, got her the job," my mother says. "You met him—the good-looking, distinguished gentleman with the *real* job, something to be proud of. I guess you've never read his reviews in *Newsday*."

Drew, without missing a beat, tells her that Howard's reviews are on the top of his list, as soon as he learns how to read.

"I only meant—" my mother starts, but both of us assure her that we know just what she meant.

"So," Drew says. "Deliveries?"

I tell him that Mario would know better than I, but that I saw vegetables come in, maybe fish and linens.

"This is the second restaurant job Howard's got her," my mother tells Drew.

"At least she's getting *something* out of the relationship," he says.

"If he were here," my mother says, ignoring the insinuation, "he'd be comforting her instead of interrogating her. He'd be making sure we're both all right after such an ordeal."

"I'm sure he would," Drew agrees, then looks me

in the eyes as if he's measuring my tolerance for shock. Quietly he adds, "But then maybe he doesn't know just what strong stuff your daughter's made of."

It's the closest thing to a tender moment I can expect from Drew Scoones. My mother breaks the spell. "She gets that from me," she says.

Both Drew and I take a minute, probably to pray that's all I inherited from her.

"I'm just trying to save you some time and effort," my mother tells him. "My money's on Howard."

Drew withers her with a look and mutters something that sounds suspiciously like "fool's gold." Then he excuses himself to go back to work.

I catch his sleeve and ask if it's all right for us to leave. He says sure, he knows where we live. I say goodbye to Mario. I assure him that I will have some sketches for him in a few days, all the while hoping that this murder doesn't cancel his redecorating plans. I need the money desperately, the alternative being borrowing from my parents and being strangled by the strings.

My mother is strangely quiet all the way to her house. She doesn't tell me what a loser Drew Scoones is—despite his good looks—and how I was obviously drooling over him. She doesn't ask me where Howard is taking me tonight or warn me not to tell my father about what happened because he will worry about us both and no doubt insist we see our respective psychiatrists.

She fidgets nervously, opening and closing her purse over and over again.

"You okay?" I ask her. After all, she's just found a dead man on the toilet and tough as she is that's got to be upsetting.

When she doesn't answer me I pull over to the side of the road.

"Mom?" She refuses to meet my eyes. "You want me to take you to see Dr. Cohen?"

She looks out the window as if she's just realized we're on Broadway in Woodmere. "Aren't we near Marvin's Jewelers?" she asks, pulling something out of her purse.

"What have you got, Mother?" I ask, prying open her fingers to find the murdered man's ring.

"It was on the sink," she says in answer to my dropped jaw. "I was going to get his name and address and have you return it to him so that he could ask you out. I thought it was a sign that the two of you were meant to be together."

"He's dead, Mom. You understand that, right?" I ask. You never can tell when my mother is fine and when she's in la-la land.

"Well, I didn't know that," she shouts at me. "Not at the time."

I ask why she didn't give it to Drew, realize that she wouldn't give Drew the time in a clock shop and add, "...or one of the other policemen?"

"For heaven's sake," she tells me. "The man is dead, Teddi, and I took his ring. How would that look?"

Before I can tell her it looks just the way it is, she pulls out a cigarette and threatens to light it.

"I mean, really," she says, shaking her head like it's my brains that are loose. "What does he need with it now?"

nocturne™

**WAS HE HER SAVIOR
OR HER NIGHTMARE?**

HAUNTED
LISA CHILDS

Years ago, Ariel and her sisters were separated for
their own protection. Now the man who vowed
revenge on her family has resumed the hunt, and
Ariel must warn her sisters before it's too late.
The closer she comes to finding them, the more
secretive her fiancé becomes. Can she trust the man
she plans to spend eternity with? Or has he been
waiting for the perfect moment to destroy her?

On sale December 2006.

SNHDEC

Silhouette®

SPECIAL EDITION™

Logan's Legacy Revisited

THE LOGAN FAMILY IS BACK
WITH SIX NEW STORIES.

Beginning in January 2007 with

THE COUPLE
MOST LIKELY TO

by

LILIAN DARCY

Tragedy drove them apart. Reunited eighteen
years later, their attraction was once again
undeniable. But had time away changed
Jake Logan enough to let him face his fears
and commit to the woman he once loved?

REQUEST YOUR FREE BOOKS!

2 FREE NOVELS PLUS 2 FREE GIFTS!

Passionate, Powerful, Provocative!

Two classic romances from
New York Times bestselling author

DEBBIE MACOMBER

Damian Dryden. *Ready for romance?* At the age of fourteen, Jessica was wildly infatuated with Evan Dryden. But that was just a teenage crush and now, almost ten years later, she's in love—truly in love—with his older brother, Damian. But everyone, including Damian, believes she's still carrying a torch for Evan.

Evan Dryden. *Ready for marriage?* Mary Jo is the woman in love with Evan. But her background's blue collar, while Evan's is blue blood. So three years ago, she got out of his life—and broke his heart. Now she needs his help. More than that, she wants his love.

The Dryden brothers—bachelors no longer. Not if these women have anything to say about it!

Ready for Love

Debbie Macomber "has a gift for evoking the emotions that are at the heart of the [romance] genre's popularity."
—*Publishers Weekly*

Available the first week of December 2006, wherever paperbacks are sold!

MIRA®

MDM2369

In February, expect **MORE** from

HARLEQUIN® *Romance*®

as it increases to six titles per month.

What's to come...

Rancher and Protector

Part of the

Western Weddings
miniseries

BY JUDY CHRISTENBERRY

The Boss's Pregnancy Proposal

BY RAYE MORGAN

Don't miss February's
incredible line up of authors!

Don't miss

DAKOTA FORTUNES,

**a six-book continuing series following
the Fortune family of South Dakota—
oil is in their blood and privilege
is their birthright.**

This series kicks off with
USA TODAY bestselling author

PEGGY MORELAND'S
Merger of Fortunes

(SD #1771)

this January.

Other books in the series:

BACK IN FORTUNE'S BED by Bronwyn James (Feb)
FORTUNE'S VENGEFUL GROOM by Charlene Sands (March)
MISTRESS OF FORTUNE by Kathie DeNosky (April)
EXPECTING A FORTUNE by Jan Colley (May)
FORTUNE'S FORBIDDEN WOMAN by Heidi Betts (June)
